G

"Have you ever thought about a night with me, with no responsibilities, no agenda and no time restrictions?"

The idea of a night with Adam stopped Kaitlyn cold. She couldn't even think straight. That was why she didn't know what to say.

"Why didn't you just call this morning? You could have given me this information over the phone or in an e-mail."

Standing this close, she could still feel everything male about him—his scent, his strength, his determination. She said weakly, "I wanted to check on Erica."

He narrowed his eyes and came so close, she could feel his breath on her cheek. "Tell the truth."

She only hesitated a moment. "I like you."

He broke into a grin. Then he kissed her—really, really hard. After he broke away, stared into her eyes for a moment, he kissed her again, this time with such coaxing passion, she wrapped her arms around his neck

It's

D0892829

A MATCH MADE
BY BABY

BY
KAREN ROSE SMITH

MILLS
BOON

Published in Great Britain 2014
by Mills & Boon, an imprint of Harlequin (UK) Limited,
Eton House, 18-24 Paradise Road, Richmond, Surrey, TW9 1SR

© 2014 Karen Rose Smith

ISBN: 978-0-263-91317-0

23-0914

Harlequin (UK) Limited's policy is to use papers that are natural, renewable and recyclable products and made from wood grown in sustainable forests. The logging and manufacturing processes conform to the legal environmental regulations of the country of origin.

Printed and bound in Spain
by Blackprint CPI, Barcelona

USA TODAY bestselling author **Karen Rose Smith**'s plots are all about emotion. She began writing in her early teens, when she listened to music and created stories to accompany the songs. An only child, she spent a lot of time in her imagination and with books—Nancy Drew, Zane Grey, *The Black Stallion* and *Anne of Green Gables*. She dreamed of brothers and sisters and a big family such as the ones her mother and father came from. This is the root of her plotlines, which include small communities and family relationships as part of everyday living. Residing in Pennsylvania with her husband and three cats, she welcomes interaction with readers on Facebook, on Twitter, @karenrosesmith, and through her website, www.karenrosesmith.com, where they can sign up for her newsletter.

To Suzanne—a terrific single mom and my BFF.
I'm grateful to have you in my life.

Chapter One

Why had *she* been on call for The Mommy Club today?

Kaitlyn Foster couldn't imagine Adam Preston in this situation to begin with. His own words from a year ago played in her ears. *I'm out of the country more than I'm in it.*

So why could she hear a baby crying on the other side of the door?

He didn't know *she* was the one coming to help.

Could there be two Adam Prestons in Fawn Grove, California? Hope sprung eternal. Maybe she wouldn't be humiliated from the top of her blond head down to her white sandals.

The baby's crying seemed to reach even higher decibels. Would he even hear the doorbell?

She pressed the button and held it down.

When Adam opened the door—and it *was* Adam—Kaitlyn found a very different Adam Preston this September morning than the debonair world traveler she'd met and almost made love with last year. This Adam's thick dark brown hair was mussed, and worry lines creased his forehead. His polo shirt looked as if it had seen a baby hiccup or two. The baby on his shoulder, who was wailing at the top of her lungs, shook the image of the expensive-suited bachelor, whose kisses had almost convinced her to sleep with a man she didn't know!

"Kaitlyn?" His intense green eyes were trying to absorb the fact she was standing at his door.

The Mommy Club was an organization that helped parents in need. "I was on call today—" She attempted to explain, but gave up and reached for the infant, who looked to be about two months old.

But instead of letting her take the baby, he took a step away. "I never imagined you worked with The Mommy Club." He patted the baby's back as if that would quiet her.

"A woman of many talents," she joked, then wished she hadn't. Adam really knew little about her except the fact she was a pediatrician. She knew little about him except for the fact that he didn't date the same woman twice. After all, she *had* looked him up on Google. And found more than she'd wanted to know.

Adam had a sister who needed his help. What else could he do but give it?

He backed away from the beautiful doctor who'd made his blood race from the moment he'd met her almost a year ago. At a wine tasting, no less. Over the past year, he'd thought about her. But he'd been in a remote part of Africa…without internet…without any connection to home except for a brief few days of R & R in Cape Town. But emailing her hadn't seemed quite right.

He sighed.

He'd emailed Tina instead, and she hadn't even told him she was pregnant.

Erica kept screaming and he cemented his focus on his niece instead of the pediatrician, who looked like a model.

Kaitlyn gave him a quick once-over, from his disheveled hair and beard stubble to his worn sneakers. The last time she'd seen him, he'd been wearing a tux, at least part of the time. "Would you like me to take her?" she asked.

The pink shirt Erica wore must have been a giveaway. She sure didn't have much hair.

Although Erica had shaken up his world, had spit up on him and generally frazzled him, he was nevertheless protective. The thought of handing her over made him uncomfortable. Kaitlyn must have seen that. "You *did* call for help, right? May I come in?"

The Mommy Club gave all kinds of help—a doctor on call, babysitting recommendations, financial assistance. He didn't need the financial assistance and he wasn't sure exactly what help he did need.

Injured pride set in. "I did call. But I didn't expect…a doctor. *You.*"

She let the "you" comment pass and glanced around again.

He understood exactly what she saw—a monumental mess. Tina had dropped the baby into his arms yesterday with a diaper bag. While he was still in shock, his sister had returned to her car and carried in a giant package of diapers, two boxes of powdered formula and a pile of one-piece outfits that he'd practically gone through already.

So dirty baby clothes were strewn from here to there. Bottles he'd washed over and over again to make sure they were clean were stationed on every tabletop. Dish towels that were spread across the sofa and chair had mopped up spills when he'd tried to burp the baby.

"Forget you *know* me," Kaitlyn said. "Let me see if I can quiet her. After all, I do have experience handling babies." Somehow she made herself heard over Erica's din and held out her hands.

Reluctantly he transferred the baby. But in the transfer, his hands brushed Kaitlyn's midriff and memories of the night they'd lingered in one of the winery's offices played much too vividly. Including the moment she'd bolted.

Maybe it was Kaitlyn's gentle smile. Maybe it was the way she held his niece so tenderly. Maybe it was simply the fact Kaitlyn Foster was a woman. But Erica's crying decreased a decibel.

Adam felt a kick in his gut. In a matter of minutes, with the doc walking and cooing, totally concentrating on the little being in her arms, Erica's cries died to whimpers.

Adam didn't know whether to swear or cheer! "How did you do that? She's been crying practically nonstop since my sister brought her here."

"It's a pediatrician's magic touch," Kaitlyn joked. She'd joked and bantered with him that night at the winery, and he remembered thinking afterward he'd liked her sense of humor.

He glanced at Erica again and saw how much more contented she seemed. "Don't all docs learn the magic touch in med school?"

"Not exactly." She studied Erica's tiny face and ran her hand down over her little body in an assessing way. "When did she eat last?"

"About an hour ago. But she wouldn't take much." He didn't know exactly how much babies were supposed to eat. He hadn't even had time to look it up on his phone. He just wished his sister had given him more information before she'd walked out.

"And before that?"

"Probably an hour before that. When she cries, I don't know what else to do. I feed her."

"Just like a new parent."

"Oh, *no!* I'm *not* a new parent."

Kaitlyn eyed him piercingly with that quick denial. "When was she changed last?"

"After I tried to feed her," he answered a bit tersely, feeling as if Kaitlyn was interrogating him.

All at once, he realized exactly what Kaitlyn was doing. With a scientific eye—he had one, too—she was sizing up the circumstances to see if they jibed with what he'd told The Mommy Club representative. She was looking over Erica as any physician would to determine if there was a medical condition underlying the crying…or something else.

Kaitlyn kept walking, seeming to take in everything again. Not simply the room and his appearance, but the overall mood, too.

He was straight with her. "I called The Mommy Club because I'm acquainted with Jase."

"He introduced us," Kaitlyn reminded him, though

he needed no reminder. Although Jase Cramer was now the general manager of Raintree Winery, he was also a photojournalist Adam had met on his work travels.

"I'd read his series about The Mommy Club on-line this summer while I had some R & R in Cape Town and could access a computer. I called the contact number today because I didn't want to bring in anyone official."

Kaitlyn's gaze met his and the room went soundless. Even Erica was silent.

"Do you have a crib or bassinet?" Kaitlyn asked.

"Her car seat is all I have to use for a bed. I was afraid she'd fall if I put her anywhere else."

A bit of a smile turned up Kaitlyn's lips, right before she sank down on the couch, holding Erica as if she was used to holding a baby. The sight made his gut tighten. That was simply because he hadn't eaten for a while, he told himself reasonably.

"Why don't you tell me why you're taking care of a baby?"

"That sounds like a social worker asking. I just wanted a little help with laundry and feeding and—"

She cut in. "You wanted a nanny?"

"Maybe. I just don't know how long my sister, Tina, will be gone, and I've never taken care of a baby before," he explained with exasperation.

As an environmental geologist, he was used to managing crews and research labs all over the world. He was *not* used to coaxing a baby to sleep.

"I'm not a social worker, Adam, but The Mommy Club *is* a responsible organization. We assess needs before we try to satisfy them."

Her gaze met his again, and he felt unsettled in

a man-woman way. Awareness. That's what it was. And he was fairly certain she felt it, too. Or else she wouldn't have responded to him the way she had when he'd kissed her. If he was honest with himself, the question of why she'd stopped him before they'd both found satisfaction had plagued him for the past year.

"Adam? Tell me how Erica ended up in your care."

There was no way around it. He'd have to give her at least *some* of the story.

"I have a sister…a stepsister. I don't see her much now. I may have told you when we met…" He trailed off, then continued. "Most of the year I'm on a job site in a foreign country. Tina and I were close once, but—" He stopped. Kaitlyn didn't need that much background. "Anyway, I just returned from Africa a week ago. That's when I found out Tina had had a baby."

"How was your sister coping a week ago?" Kaitlyn obviously wanted to get to the heart of the matter.

"She seemed frazzled. She lives in Sacramento, and we'd made plans to get together. If only I'd realized what was going on with her—"

Kaitlyn jumped right in. "What would have been different? Would you have given up your job and come home?"

Tough questions. Would he have done that? Or would he have tried to get her help some other way?

Erica stirred again and gave a little cry. After Kaitlyn readjusted the baby in her arms, she quieted.

"Would you like some coffee?" Adam asked, wanting to take charge again in some way. Besides, he needed the caffeine. Staying awake was all-important with a baby around.

"Coffee would be great," Kaitlyn admitted with a smile that sparked a longing inside Adam. One he didn't understand. Then she added, "I'd like to hear more about Tina."

Fine. She wanted the whole story—he'd give it to her.

Although Kaitlyn made home visits with The Mommy Club occasionally, she did not become personally involved…for lots of very good reasons. She hadn't confided any of *her* background to Adam. The chemistry between them had just seemed to trump everything else. The night they'd met she hadn't quite been herself and had acted in a way that was out of character for her. Way out of character.

As Adam prepared coffee, she took another good look at the condo. Yep, a baby had taken over his world. But underneath that surface mess, she saw a bachelor pad. Chrome and glass and shiny black leather sent the message that a cleaning service might see the inside of Adam's living room more often than he did. She noticed the lack of photographs.

Peeking into the kitchen, her tummy did a little somersault when she stared at his broad shoulders, his dark brown mussed hair, his tall lean frame.

Erica stirred again. With a baby in her arms, Kaitlyn was transported back to a time when her own dreams were still a possibility. She slid her finger along the infant's cheek. The little girl was almost asleep. To put her down or let her nap in her arms?

Adam solved that dilemma. As he entered the living room with two mugs in hand, he said, "Maybe she'll sleep in her car seat now," in a low voice, as if afraid to bring Erica's crying to life again.

The fact that his sister had brought the baby in in her car seat was at least a sign she had Erica's welfare at heart. "Let's give it a try. We can set it right here on the floor as we talk."

His frown told her talking wasn't high on his priority list. Because sharing made him uncomfortable? Or because he had something to hide?

Adam set her mug on the glass table beside the sofa. "Do you need milk or sugar? I'm not sure I have sugar—"

"Black is fine. Caffeine is a daily necessity. I'm a doctor, remember?"

"Oh, I remember," he said as he crossed to the kitchen.

When he returned, he set the car seat on the floor between them. Kaitlyn easily transferred Erica to it then let her finger trail down the infant's cheek once more.

"Babies can burrow a tunnel straight into your heart, and you don't even know they've done it," she murmured. Her practice had taught her that.

The silence in the living room with Erica quiet and their conversation at a standstill brought her gaze to Adam's.

His serious green eyes seemed to see too much, but then he said, "I wouldn't know. This is the first I've been around one."

A bit flustered, she quickly picked up her coffee mug. The brew was almost black—the way she liked it.

"Weren't you around your sister when she was a

baby?" He'd given her a lead in to his background, so she took it.

"As I said, Tina's my stepsister, and you're going to poke around until you learn all about us, aren't you?" He certainly wasn't happy about it.

"Why does that bother you?"

"Because I like to keep my private life private."

"So do I."

He must have seen the truth behind that declaration because his defensively tense broad shoulders relaxed. "This is just your job," he reminded himself.

"I like to think of it as a vocation." She stared down at Erica, remembering her own pregnancy and the baby she lost. Giving herself a mental shake, she said, "Tell me when Tina came into your life."

A myriad of memories seemed to pass through Adam Preston's eyes, and she realized this was a man who could feel...if he'd let himself.

He took a few swallows of coffee as if to fortify himself. "This isn't easy," he told Kaitlyn.

"Isn't easy, because it's painful to remember?" she guessed.

"Not painful. It was just a rough time. Tina and I never talk about it."

Erica began to wake up, and he said, "Maybe this should wait."

"I can't give you any help if this waits. Do you have a bottle? Let's try to feed her. Maybe this time she'll eat."

"And if she doesn't?"

"Then we'll figure out the next best thing to do."

Scooping Erica from her car seat, Kaitlyn stood,

and Adam moved close to her. So close her gaze went to his lips and she swallowed hard.

"I'll take her," he said, and that surprised Kaitlyn.

"Are you sure?"

"I fed her all through the night, and tried this morning. I've got to succeed at something about this."

So Adam Preston wasn't a man who accepted failure. She recognized the same quality in herself. He'd either seen too much of it in his life, or not enough.

The exchange of the baby was awkward. His hand slid close to Kaitlyn's breast. If she could have thought of it as merely a clinical move, it wouldn't have bothered her at all. But everything about this situation seemed personal.

It's not personal, she chastised herself.

Adam slid his arm around the baby. But when he brought Erica close, his shoulder rubbed Kaitlyn's. At that point, their gazes met.

The room developed a certain buzz, but then Kaitlyn hadn't had any breakfast this morning. A half cup of dark, rich coffee, with lots of caffeine streaming through her veins would be enough to make her feel a little unnerved.

After the baby successfully found Adam's arms again, he brought her up to his face and cooed to her. None of this was contrived. Adam must have figured out Erica liked that last night.

"So you want me to warm the bottle?" Kaitlyn asked, feeling disconcerted. How could a bachelor who serial dated be good at holding a baby? "She seems pretty satisfied right now."

"You don't mind?"

"I did come to help," she said with a wink, knowing this was the kind of help he'd expected.

A few minutes later, Kaitlyn returned with the bottle. "If she doesn't take the formula, we might have to change it."

"I have to go to the store," he admitted. "She needs a lot of things, and a crib's one of them."

"Let's get her basic needs settled first, then we can take care of that."

Kaitlyn saw his brows go up when she said "we," but she meant The Mommy Club—the community of parents who wanted to help "we," the all-inclusive "we." Not a her-and-Adam "we." The idea of her and Adam together in any way gave her goose bumps.

"I'm going to have to get a rocker," he decided. "I think she'd like that while she's eating or falling asleep."

While Erica sucked on the bottle, Kaitlyn said, "You were going to tell me about when you met Tina."

He closed his eyes for a moment and took a deep breath. Then he revealed, "I was fourteen and she was three. My dad was a widower. He met this waitress where he often had breakfast and they ended up getting married. She was a lot younger than my mom."

"And that made you uncomfortable?"

"It made me realize Dad was going to put all of his attention toward his second family—his young wife and a three-year-old who was as cute as a button."

"So how did you feel about *her?*" Resentment would have been natural.

But Adam gave her a wry smile. "Tina had these big gray eyes and straight blond hair. When she looked up at you, your heart just melted. I felt like a big brother instantly, very protective. Especially protective when my dad and Jade divorced. Tina was only eight and didn't understand anything that was happening. She'd come to me and cry and cry and cry. That year I'd graduated and I was off to college. I kept in touch with Tina, though. We emailed regularly. She came to visit me now and then with her mom. She had a really tough time again two years ago while Jade battled ovarian cancer. So Tina's been through a lot."

"It sounds as if you were there to help."

"When I wasn't there physically, I still tried to support her. There were lots of nights we instant messaged when her mom was dying. Fortunately then I was in a part of Alaska that wasn't too remote."

"Do you think all of that's caught up with Tina?"

"Possibly. She has a good heart, Kaitlyn. But she's twenty-two…and still young. From what she's told me, Erica's father has left for parts unknown. She's feeling overwhelmed. I've got to find her, bring her back here and get her help."

"Have you thought about the possibility that she won't be coming back?"

"No." His firm denial said he'd make sure she came back, one way or another.

"Adam." She had to put this as gently as possible. "If your sister doesn't want to be a mother, you can't force her to be."

His determination was evident in his expression. "I can't force her to be, but I can set things up to make it easier for her to *be* a mother. Apparently, I haven't done enough, and I intend to remedy that. But right now I have a baby to take care of."

He took the bottle from the baby's mouth and raised

her to his shoulder to burp her, but she didn't burp. She spit up and started crying.

If Adam thought he could learn to be a substitute dad in twenty-four hours or even a few days, he was sadly mistaken.

Chapter Two

A half hour later, Kaitlyn walked beside Adam through the department store. She'd offered to come along because even the best parents sometimes had difficulty juggling a baby and shopping. However, whenever she got within a foot of him, chemistry seemed to snap, crackle and pop between them.

Just like that night at Raintree Winery.

Jase and Adam had been talking. She'd been on her way to speak to Jase's wife, Sara, when Jase had called to her and introduced Adam.

When she'd lifted her gaze to Adam's—

Something had happened that had made the air buzz between them. Maybe that buzz had drowned out her good sense. Or maybe since her divorce had just become final, she'd had something to prove—that she was still attractive and desirable.

They'd talked for a half hour while they tasted one Raintree wine after another. Yes, she had to admit she'd flirted with him. What breathing woman wouldn't have? He was Mr. Tall, Dark and So-o-o Sexy.

The event had become more crowded and they found it hard to hear each other, so they'd wandered down the hall and settled in an office with a long burgundy leather couch. Adam had closed the door so they'd have privacy…to talk.

They *had* talked. Mostly about sites Adam had seen in his travels as an environmental geologist… how she'd been homeschooled before it had become more common because she'd been academically ahead of all her peers, gone to college at sixteen and fought her way through med school because she was younger than everyone else. But her determination and dedication paid off. And then—

Adam had said, "I never expected to meet a woman like you tonight."

In her professional life, she was confident. But her divorce had shaken her personal confidence in so many ways. And to hear that from Adam's deep voice—

"You're beautiful, sexy and dedicated to what you do."

Her ex-husband had considered that dedication a flaw, especially at the end of their marriage. "Thank you," she'd murmured, never taking her gaze from his.

That's when he'd kissed her, and she'd responded as if her life had depended on it.

The kiss expanded, catching both of them in its web. They kissed again and again. She'd hardly noticed Adam unfastening her blouse. His hand on her breast had been so arousing. She'd unbuttoned his shirt, felt his hot skin and springy brown hair. When his hand ventured between her thighs and cupped her, she'd reached for his belt.

But then she'd heard voices in the hall. Gazing up at Adam, she'd glimpsed the hungry desire in his eyes.

"What's wrong?" he'd asked.

She'd panicked. She was almost naked, lying under a man she didn't even know!

She'd slid away from him, scrambled to a sitting position, avoided his gaze and buttoned her blouse. "I can't do this. I should never have let this happen!"

And then she'd bolted, leaving Adam sitting there. She'd rushed out of the winery, wondering what in blazes had gotten into her, wondering why she'd been reckless when she'd never done anything like that before.

Now Kaitlyn hurried to keep up with Adam's long strides to the baby department. In the year since she'd met him at the winery, she'd thought about him. But she hadn't had any means of contacting him in a remote location.

When Erica made a noise, Adam stopped and looked down at her as if…as if he cared.

Could this bad boy—after all, she'd researched him after their "encounter"—who traveled the world, really care about an infant? An infant who wasn't even his?

Glancing up at her, seeing that she was watching him, Adam looked disconcerted. Then his expression changed, and he didn't look disconcerted as much as he looked determined. "We should talk about what happened the last time we were together."

Uh-oh. Maybe his mind *had* been wandering in the same direction. "This isn't a good place," she said calmly. Her heart sped up, and she knew she didn't want to have that discussion at all, let alone *here*.

His jaw set and his gaze was just a little too penetrating. "That's an excuse—I'll settle for it for now, at least until we get everything we need for Erica.... What do we need?"

At the baby section now, Kaitlyn pointed to a big box on the lower shelf. "You need a swing."

He looked at her as if she were crazy.

"Really," she assured him. "Erica fell asleep in the car. That means she likes motion. So if you want any peace, you should give her motion." She pointed to the picture on the box.

Adam crouched down to look at it more closely. The overhead lights glimmered on russet strands in his hair, thick dark hair she'd run her fingers through. His shoulders were wider than the box he was studying. Those shoulders had felt tautly muscled under her hands. He was so long-waisted, with a runner's legs. He'd told her he jogged wherever he happened to be. She remembered the pressure of his lower body on top of hers. His jeans fit him too well. Although his shirt was loose, as he crouched down like that, examining the box, it molded to his back.

Although it had been over a year, she hadn't been able to dismiss the picture of the two of them entwined in each other's arms. It had haunted her dreams.

He grabbed one of the boxes, easily lifted it, and stowed it on the bottom of their cart. "It doesn't look too complicated. In fact, it makes me wonder if the company should make them for adults."

She couldn't help but smile at the wryness in his tone. "I've often thought I'd like a swing on my front porch. That's if I ever have a front porch."

"Where do you live now?"

"I rent a town house—no maintenance, no upkeep, no porch."

He studied her as if he were searching for meaning under her words. "I suppose you're not home much."

"If I'm not at my office, I'm doing volunteer work for The Mommy Club. That doesn't leave spare time to plant a garden."

"I know what you mean," Adam said. "But sometimes I wonder what normal life would be like."

"Normal?"

"Yeah, you know. A nine-to-five job, leisure time in the evenings, regular weekends. If I had a normal life…if I hadn't been out of the country…" He motioned to Erica. "Maybe I would have seen what was happening with Tina."

The work he did for a private consulting firm out of Sacramento sounded important. The night they'd met, he'd explained that he traveled the world doing research helping countries put in water systems. Before…before they'd ended up in each other's arms on that couch.

Pushing that memory aside once more, she took this opportunity to get firsthand knowledge of his life. "You come and go as you please. You travel to exotic places. That would be hard to give up."

"Yes, it would," he admitted. "I don't like to feel trapped, tied down, tethered to one place. That brings back memories of—" He stopped, and she could see he wasn't going to go on.

What did he run from in his mind? What kept him on the move? Searching for something that would satisfy him? She knew what would satisfy *her,* yet it seemed impossible and out of her reach.

Gazing down at Erica, she suddenly wondered if she should adopt a child. Why not forget about relationships and the marriage part.

The silence between them grew awkward, and Kaitlyn reached for a contraption hanging on a hook. "This is something else you need."

"I'm afraid to ask what it is," he said in a wry tone.

She looked at Erica and saw that her eyes were wide-open. "It's as good a time as any to try this out." She gave it to Adam and said, "Hang this part around your neck."

Adam did as she suggested, looking wary.

Scooping Erica from her car seat, Kaitlyn placed her in the sling, close to Adam's chest. She had to touch his chest and that reminded her of touching it once before. When her fingers brushed against him, the look in his eyes said he remembered, too.

"I can get it," he decided, taking a step away from her. "Now that I think about it, I've seen women wearing these."

"Daddies, too," she assured him. "That keeps Erica close to your body heat, and she feels more secure."

Their eyes met. She remembered *his* body heat, feeling secure, but so much more, too.

"Kaitlyn!" She was never so glad to hear her name called.

She knew the voice, and it was a welcome relief, interrupting the too-knowing moment between her and Adam. She turned and saw her friend Marissa Lopez strolling down the aisle, her one-year-old sitting in the basket kicking his legs.

She gave them both a wide smile. "Hi, Marissa." She went over to Jordan and tickled his tummy. "And how are you, big boy?"

He grinned at her and stuck a finger in his mouth. Kaitlyn had babysat Jordan many times. "What are you doing here?"

"I needed diapers again," Marissa added, brushing her black curls away from her face.

Kaitlyn introduced Adam and said, "Marissa works at Raintree Winery."

"Jase is your boss?" Adam asked.

Marissa nodded with a wide smile. "Yes. More than that, really. He and Sara have become good friends."

"I met Jase when we crossed paths in Africa a few years ago."

"That's when he was photographing children in refugee camps?" Kaitlyn asked.

Adam nodded. "I was in the area with a humanitarian group that was trying to bring safe water to some of the villages."

Erica gave a little cry, and Marissa came over to her. "What a sweetie. Is she about two months old?"

"About," Adam confirmed. "She's my sister's baby. I'm taking care of her for a while. The Mommy Club sent Kaitlyn to give me a few instructions."

That was one way of putting it, Kaitlyn supposed.

"The Mommy Club's been a lifesaver for me, too," Marissa told him. "I'm a single mom and they've been a great help. We all try to give back when we can. Sara is watching Jordan while I volunteer at Thrifty Solutions, The Mommy Club thrift store, tomorrow night."

"I'm there on Monday evening," Kaitlyn said.

Adam eyed Jordan. "Is he walking yet?"

"Oh, yes, and running. He helps me get my exercise every day."

They all laughed and Adam shook his head. "I've learned respect for all new moms."

Marissa checked her watch. "I have to get going. I had the morning off because I worked some long hours last week. But now I have to take Jordan to day care and get to the winery." She studied Adam and Erica. "Good luck. If you have Kaitlyn advising you, you will be okay."

After a hug for Kaitlyn, she wheeled her cart away.

"So she's a single mom?" Adam asked reflectively as they watched Marissa walk away. He was trying to put himself in his sister's place, trying to imagine what she'd been thinking and feeling before she'd left.

"Yes, she is."

"And you became friends because of The Mommy Club?" He'd imagined The Mommy Club was mostly a group of women looking out for each other. It was a nice concept really.

"We did."

"I don't see how you have time for it all."

"I think we all make time for what we want to do."

He wondered if The Mommy Club filled a need Kaitlyn had to help and nurture. What did that need come from? He found he was awfully curious about her and wanted to know.

He pointed to a portable crib. "I guess I'll get one of those, too. I can donate it to The Mommy Club when Tina returns. I'm sure she'll be back before the week's out."

Kaitlyn stood a little closer so their conversation was private. "It could be longer than a week. If your sister is in the throes of postpartum depression, she might need a doctor's help to emerge from it."

Adam's brow furrowed. "How am I going to get her help when she won't answer my calls?"

"All you can do is hope that she contacts you soon."

"I have to do more than hope. I'm supposed to be on a plane to Thailand in a month."

Erica started crying, and Adam's arms went around her with a protective gesture, but it didn't help.

"If you're tense and upset, it can affect her. Babies pick up moods."

He exhaled, took Erica out of the sling and laid her in her car seat. "Maybe she's hungry again. Let's get what we need and head back to the condo."

Taking care of Erica was complicated enough. Tackling the vibrations between him and Kaitlyn added to the unnerving situation.

Once he had everything he needed for his niece, Kaitlyn would be out of his life once more.

Back at Adam's condo, Kaitlyn watched Adam as he held and walked Erica and readied a bottle with the new formula she'd chosen. Four hands were better than two in this kind of situation.

She asked, "Would you like me to feed her?"

He shook his head. "No. I have to learn how to do this and do it right." He took the bottle from Kaitlyn, their fingers brushing. They avoided each other's gazes, and he went to the living room, this time sitting in the armchair.

And to her dismay, he was still as sexy as could

be—a six-foot-two, broad-shouldered, handsome man feeding a baby intently. Her heart gave a little trip. Erica was greedily sucking on the nipple, and Adam looked as if he'd conquered the world.

"If this formula is better suited to her, she might start sleeping for you," Kaitlyn assured him.

"That's an awfully big 'if' and 'might.'"

"There are never any guarantees with babies."

"How come you don't have a slew of your own? You seem to really love children."

The stark sincerity in his question took her breath away. Usually sure of herself, right now, she didn't know how to answer him.

He must have realized something was wrong, because he looked up from the baby, and his gaze met hers. "Kaitlyn?"

Their evening together and what had almost happened between them flashed before her eyes again. It seemed to require some kind of honesty, though she didn't know why. But she couldn't be honest with this man. She didn't really know him.

So she fell back on the usual excuse. "I work so many hours—"

Suddenly, a beeping came from Adam's hip. It was his phone. "That could be Tina," he said with some desperation in his voice.

Kaitlyn stood immediately and scooped Erica from his arms. Her hand brushed against his chest, and she could feel his hardness under the material of his shirt. She knew there was springy, dark brown hair there. But she concentrated on the baby and the bottle and settling on the sofa with Erica to feed her some more while he took his call.

He checked the screen. "Not Tina. It's my father. He might know where she is."

"Hello, Dad," he said with a little more distance than Kaitlyn would expect between father and son.

She unabashedly listened, curious about Adam's family connections.

"Where are you?" Adam asked.

He paused for an obvious few moments of explanation.

"So you're in Ireland, but you plan to fly to England tomorrow?"

His father must have agreed that was the plan because Adam asked, "Have you heard from Tina at all?"

A short answer there, most likely no.

"Something's happened, Dad. She's not herself. I think she ran off and left Erica with me because she's depressed and needs help."

His father must have said something.

"I was out of the country. Didn't find out she'd had a baby until I got home. I need to find her, and maybe instead of taking a jaunt to England, you should come home."

Another pause. "I know you promised Iris you'd take her to Ireland and Scotland and everything in between, but this is a family emergency. *Our* family emergency. Jade's gone and Tina has no one else. You and I, in the past few years, have practically deserted her. Of course she feels like she doesn't have any support. You're out of the country. I was out of the country. How often do we call her? How often does she call us? And what kind of example are either of us setting for her? You've been married four times—"

He stopped abruptly and glanced at Kaitlyn. His fa-

ther must have made some retort because Adam shook
his head and clenched his jaw. "I might be a serial
dater, but you're a serial groom. If you hear from Tina,
day or night, anytime, call me. This is important, Dad.
I have a group of people here who will help her."

His father must have asked him a question.

Adam answered, "I'm leaving for Thailand in a
month. I have no choice. This is a contracted commitment. If that means you have to come back and
babysit for a while, that's what it means."

Adam just kept shaking his head at the rest of the
conversation.

After he ended the call, he slowly slipped the phone
back into the holster on his belt, looking as if he'd
gone far away.

"It didn't go well?"

Adam gave a mirthless laugh. "No, it didn't. But
that's not unusual with Dad. He's always been more
concerned about his most recent marriage to Tiffany
or Anna Mae or whoever comes next. But Tina and
I—we were pretty much on our own. We never understood why he and Jade divorced. They never told us."

"It seems you watched over Tina a lot when you
were younger. Didn't you mind having a tagalong?
That had to cramp your style given the big age difference."

"I didn't have a style. I studied mostly. I ran track,
but only so I could get a scholarship."

Adam's pride was almost as big as he was. The
stiffness in his voice concealed his true feelings. She
imagined they would have been sorrow, loneliness and
regret. However, just as she hadn't confided in him,
she could tell he wasn't going to confide in her. She

knew about the arrest he'd had when he was twenty-one…that his younger years hadn't been all studies and sports, even though that's what he wanted her to think. He'd been involved in a serious accident that had been *his* fault.

However, she didn't push further. She didn't want to get more involved than she already was. "So your dad didn't know Tina was pregnant?"

"No. I called and left a message for him yesterday after Tina left Erica with me. We're a pair, the two of us."

"But not alike. You haven't been married four times."

Adam gave her a penetrating stare. "No, I haven't been married four times. But I also haven't had a serious relationship with a woman for more than a couple of months. Make that one month. I guess I come from a gene pool that can't commit."

"You think it's in the genes?"

"I think it's in the genes, and I think you have to grow up in the right atmosphere. I batted zilch on both."

"I don't agree."

When he studied her at her remark, she knew he'd never expected her to contradict him.

"Just what don't you agree with?" he asked. "You don't know what my childhood was like."

"No, I don't. But I do know we do what we want to do—when we're kids and when we're adults. Granted, it's easier if someone teaches us how to get along with other people. But basically, I think if we want a friend, we make a friend. If we want a mate, we look for the possibilities—which could be anything from a one-night stand to a lasting commitment. But we have to *want* it, Adam."

"How do you know what I want? Seems to me, you didn't stick around to find out." He sounded regretful about that and she wondered why. After all, he'd just admitted he didn't date anyone longer than a month!

"I knew what you wanted that night, just as you knew what you wanted. But I—"

"You chickened out, and I'd like to know why."

Oh, there it was. The conversation that she didn't want to have.

Taking the bottle away from the baby, she said calmly, "I have to burp her. Do you want to learn how?"

"Kaitlyn, you're cutting it off again."

"I'm not here to discuss what happened a year ago. I'm here to figure out what's best for this baby. Do you want to learn to burp her?"

Adam's brow furrowed, his jaw set, and she saw the storms in his eyes. He was used to being in control. He was used to being in charge. And right now, he wasn't.

"Show me what to do, and you won't have to show me how to do it again."

Well, those lines were drawn.

Kaitlyn lifted Erica and took her over to Adam. She said, "Sit up straight. You *can* burp a baby on your shoulder, but you said that wasn't working for you. So we'll try something else. I'm going to sit her on your knee."

Kaitlyn knelt down beside Adam so she could more easily help. "Support her back like I'm doing."

When Adam transferred his hand to Erica's back,

Kaitlyn's was still there. She slipped hers away, but not without feeling the warmth of his long fingers.

"Now you're going to put your other hand in front of Erica and let her weight rest against your palm." Kaitlyn was almost between Adam's knees now, and it was uncomfortable and awkward, yet also an exciting place to be, if she was honest with herself.

If he brushed his cheek against hers from this vantage point, she'd feel his stubble. She could remember the feel of his lips on hers, the tempting mastery of his tongue, the passion he'd evoked that had almost swept her away.

Inhaling a deep breath, and along with it his musky scent, she believed this was the worst assignment she'd ever had from The Mommy Club. When she'd learned the person who needed help was Adam Preston, she should have called one of the other docs to help.

Crazy, but she was feeling a little crazy right now. So close to Adam, yet emotionally removed. At least she was trying to be.

"Let her lean into your palm, and just rub her back. That's all you have to do. You can pat it a little, too, but—"

Erica gave a loud burp, and the formula stayed down.

Kaitlyn gave a little smile then moved away, now that she felt Adam was more confident in what he was doing.

They were still too close. She realized the best thing she could do was leave.

She rose to her feet. "I'd better be going. I have to check on a patient at the hospital in Sacramento."

"Leave?" he asked with a pointed look. He nodded toward the boxed swing and the crib. "I suppose I could put those together while she sleeps, *if* she sleeps. What have you decided about the situation here? Can you send somebody out to help?"

Actually, The Mommy Club was shorthanded right now. There were several members of the community who needed help. One young mother had had surgery. Another was undergoing chemo for breast cancer, and several women were helping take care of her children and bring in food. Sometimes it seemed like The Mommy Club had a score of volunteers. But when it came down to the nitty-gritty, daily help was hard to find.

Adam must have seen something in her face. "What? No one's available? Or are you just going to call a social worker and say I'm not fit to take care of Erica?"

"That wouldn't be the truth. But I really don't know the answer yet. I'll check back with you tomorrow. You'll be fine. I know you will."

"I'll be fine," he agreed. "But I don't think *you're* fine, Kaitlyn, because you're running. I don't know why, and you obviously don't want to tell me, but you're running. Think about that while you're driving to Sacramento."

Kaitlyn knew she'd think about nothing else.

Chapter Three

In the Sacramento hospital, Kaitlyn kept her attention focused on her four-year-old patient who was doing much better. She was grateful for that. The little girl had been mighty sick, and Kaitlyn hadn't let that worry show to the parents.

But now as she read Mary Lou's chart on her electronic tablet, she was hopeful her patient would be going home soon.

She'd just turned away from the nurses' desk when she heard her name called. Valerie Tremont waved from the sitting area. She had a cup of coffee beside her and Kaitlyn guessed she was taking a break. A nurse here, Val had been keeping to herself lately, and Kaitlyn suspected why. A divorce. Kaitlyn knew firsthand how that could tear up a person's life.

Glad for any distraction from Adam and his niece, Kaitlyn approached Val with a smile. "How are you?"

"Surviving," she said with an attempt at cheerfulness.

"Are Chrissy and Craig okay?"

"We're all adjusting. It's not as if David had been home the past few years."

Her husband, David, had been a medic in the marines and deployed several times. Over a year ago, he'd decided to walk away from his marriage. Although Val lived in Fawn Grove, she worked at the hospital in Sacramento because the pay and benefits were better than anything she could find locally.

"Do you see David?"

Val shook her head. "After that last deployment, his discharge and the divorce, he said he just needed time for himself. The last I heard, he was taking a hostel trip through Spain. I think he just saw too much in his service, and he's trying to escape the memories."

Kaitlyn sat down beside her. "How's the apartment working out?"

"The Mommy Club did a great job recommending one. It's on the first floor of an old house. I still don't have an upstairs neighbor, which is nice because the kids have the run of the yard anytime they want it. And I can't believe how reasonable the rent is. I think my next goal is to find a job nursing in Fawn Grove so I don't have to commute. Mom and Dad need a life, too, outside of babysitting."

"I'll keep my ears open."

"Thank you. How are *you?*"

Today she was a bit disconcerted, but other than that… "I'm good."

"Are you going to The Mommy Club fund-raiser at Raintree Winery next week?"

Kaitlyn had to smile. "The bachelor auction? I don't know. I'll help Sara and Jase get the word out, but the event itself isn't quite my cup of tea."

Because the thought of a dinner date threw her into a tizzy? She'd never been much of a dater, not with her med school workload and meeting Tom. When she looked back at her marriage, she wondered if she and Tom had settled for each other because it had been convenient, because they'd both wanted a family. But her miscarriage and the reason behind it had ended that possibility in Tom's mind.

"Are *you* going to the fund-raiser?" Kaitlyn asked with a twinkle in her eye.

"No," Val returned with a firm shake of her head. "I don't know when I'll be able to think about dating again."

"You need more time."

"And a fairy godmother," Val said with a laugh.

Did all women really have dreams of finding Prince Charming? On that score, Kaitlyn's dreams had dissolved into something much more practical—a thriving practice where she could help the kids she saw every day. She didn't need anything else.

However, as Kaitlyn was driving back to Fawn Grove, she felt an inexorable pull toward Adam's condo to see how he was faring with his niece. After all, she'd told him she'd check in on him. She told *herself* that picking up some Chinese on the way was mostly for her sustenance. She'd skipped lunch. She'd also told herself as she rang the doorbell, chemistry and a doctor's busy lifestyle simply didn't mix.

That maxim held water until Adam opened the

door. This time he was wearing the baby sling with Erica in it, but his niece was wailing again.

Adam seemed unreasonably glad to see Kaitlyn, yet unsettled, too. Was he pleased she was here to help? Or because...

Or because he couldn't forget about their kisses, either?

Without preamble, he said, "A mother wearing this contraption and me wearing this contraption are entirely two different things."

"Do you want me to come in, or do you want me to leave with my Moo Goo Gai Pan?"

"Moo Goo Gai Pan?" The thought of hot food was the one thing that might bring him a little pleasure. Well, maybe there was more than one thing that would, but they'd concentrate on the food.

"Sweet and sour chicken, too," she added.

He had to wonder why she was doing this. After all, she'd run away before. "So now The Mommy Club delivers takeout?"

"So now a pediatrician with The Mommy Club was hungry and thought you might be, too. I didn't see much food in your refrigerator."

He didn't have a comeback to that remark because it was true. He simply crossed into his living room where the swing stood, leaving her to close the door behind her. "The swing worked for about fifteen minutes." As he transferred Erica from the sling to the swing, his gaze found Kaitlyn's.

Darn if the room didn't tilt again. Mini earthquake?

Although the aroma from the food was making his mouth water, he couldn't take his eyes from Kaitlyn's.

Whenever she was around, his head practically spun. Or maybe that was just a lack of sleep.

With a mental shake, he settled Erica in the padded seat and cooed a bit to her as he wound up the mechanism so the swing would swing. For some reason his niece seemed to like cooing and gooing. Babies were as tough to read as women.

"I hope you brought your magic touch with you," he suddenly said, "or that food's going to get cold. I'm paying you, by the way."

She looked startled, as if she hadn't expected the offer. "You can pay me *if* you get the chance to eat any of it. We can split the cost."

That made him straighten from his crouch and study her carefully. "You're one complicated woman."

Her eyes widened a bit. "And you're an open book? One thing I'm not, Mr. Preston, is gullible."

"Mr. Preston," he scoffed. "After what we almost did, first name basis should be a given. So don't try to put even more distance than the past year between us."

Kaitlyn looked away, obviously not wanting to have that discussion *now*. But he did. If not now, then soon. He had to know what had made her bolt like a scared rabbit.

Erica seemed to be quieting with each pass of the swing.

"If we only have fifteen minutes, we should take advantage of it," he decided. "I'll find dishes. Some of each?"

She raised her hand in a "sure, why not" gesture. As she followed him into the kitchen, she asked, "Did you get the crib put together?"

"Who do you think I am? Superman?"

The way she studied him made him wonder if she was imagining him in that superhero getup.

A short while later, they were sitting on the sofa quietly eating their supper, the swing rocking back and forth, easing Erica into sleep, when Kaitlyn asked Adam what was foremost on her mind. "Did you try to call Tina again?"

He put down his fork. "Three times. I don't even know if she's getting my messages. I try not to sound panicked. I try to sound reasonable. But I'm worried about her."

"I know you are."

It was obvious to see, though she wondered how much of it was worry that he'd be stuck with Erica. She was afraid that's the way he looked at it. She couldn't tell yet if Adam was bonding with the baby, or just caring for her. There was a difference.

As they ate in silence for another few minutes, Kaitlyn took a deep breath. Having dinner with Adam wasn't as easy as she'd thought it would be. That sizzle in the air…the way he looked at her sometimes…

"I'm going to drive to Tina's apartment tomorrow," he said, breaking the silence. "Maybe I'll find a clue as to where she's gone."

"You're taking Erica?"

"What choice do I have? Besides, I have to learn to handle her in and out of the condo. I can't be stuck here twenty-four hours a day. No wonder new moms get cabin fever."

"There's no reason why Erica can't go where you go. You just have to remember to take along everything you need."

"Bottles, diapers and the kitchen sink."

At least he was keeping his sense of humor. That could be tough in this situation. She'd liked his sense of humor that night—

"Kaitlyn, why did you run out on me that night at the winery?"

Back to that. "Because we didn't know each other. Because we'd just met."

"Did I read the signals wrong? You were flirting back. When I kissed you, you responded."

She'd more than responded. Somehow, he'd lit the wick of passion that had been extinguished for two years. Her divorce had become final the week before.

Yes, she'd realized that Tom would never forgive her for losing their baby. She'd had no doubt the marriage was over. The night she'd gone to the wine tasting, she'd been trying to resurrect her own self-confidence. Whatever her goal that night, she hadn't expected to meet Adam. She hadn't expected that kind of chemistry. She hadn't expected to go up in flames when he touched her.

But now she could see why he wanted to have this conversation. A dented male ego, maybe, but something deeper, too. He was afraid he'd taken advantage of her.

"You didn't read the signals wrong, Adam. I thought I could flirt and have a good time. I didn't expect everything that happened when you kissed me. After we ended up undressing and I realized what we were doing, I knew I wasn't ready."

Of course, that's the word he latched on to. "Ready?"

"That's all I really want to say about it. You didn't

take advantage of me. I never should have let you kiss
me the second time."

He cocked his head and studied her hard. "You
don't go to many parties, do you?"

"No."

"You don't usually flirt with men."

"No."

"So why that night? Why me?"

Wasn't that a very good question? She knew why
she'd done it that night, but why she'd done it with
Adam was still a puzzle.

"Maybe it was because Jase introduced us. I'm not
sure."

"Something happened," he guessed.

"Adam, that's enough. I don't want to talk about
it. If I could have gotten another doctor to come this
morning, I would have."

"To avoid an awkward situation." He was trying
out that statement to see if it sounded true.

"Yes."

"Or…to avoid the idea you might still be attracted
to me if you saw me again."

"No."

"You answered that one much too quickly. Maybe
you need to think about it a little more."

She pushed her food around on her plate. "I don't
need to think about it at all. I'm not looking for a relationship. And if I were, it wouldn't be with someone
like you," she said honestly.

"Someone like *me,* meaning what?"

"Someone who's never around. You said yourself
you don't believe in commitment, that family life isn't

something you even know. We'd be incompatible, from start to finish."

"It depends on what we'd be starting, and what we'd be finishing."

His words on their own weren't seductive, but they made her blush, because the underlying message was clear. He was thinking about sex.

"Tell me your fondest dream for five years from now," he suggested.

She never thought that far ahead anymore, not in her personal life. "I don't have that dream worked out."

"I think you do. Close your eyes."

"Adam."

"Do as I say. Close your eyes."

So she did.

"Five years from now, where are you living?"

That stopped her for a few seconds, and then she realized this was a dream. "Somewhere outside of town where I'd have some open space. I want a fireplace for cold nights that I can sit in front of with someone I love, and a porch that would be large enough for a very nice swing that my kids could enjoy, too."

"How can that ever happen if you're too busy with your practice and The Mommy Club doesn't leave much time for parties or a social life?"

Her eyes popped open.

"Your goals are divided. On one hand you want to save the world, on the other you want to find somebody to love."

"Adam, you don't know me. We had…what? A half-hour conversation?"

"And a half-hour make-out session. Do you think I can't tell from that how a woman feels, what she might find important? We did talk, Kaitlyn. It wasn't earth-shatteringly personal. But we talked. And believe it or not, I listened. You enjoy being part of a group practice, not only because you're not always on call, but because you have camaraderie."

He *had* been listening. He didn't stop there. "Jase introduced us because he said you and his wife were good friends. He pointed to the wine you liked best and said I might like to try it, too. When we tasted it together, you said you like visiting Raintree, walking through the vineyards—"

She held up her hand, like the stop sign it was meant to be. "All right. You proved you listen."

"Did *you?*" he asked.

Uh-oh. Her mind had been filled with regrets and recriminations that night, wanting to prove herself in a way she hadn't in a long time. Just how much did she remember from before their kiss?

"Jase mentioned you met him in Kenya, that the famine wasn't the only problem, that the water in the refugee camp was tainted and the children were getting sick from that, too. You were trying to find a good water supply and convinced the villagers that your team could engineer it."

"Score one for you," Adam said, as if he expected no less.

"You also said you were on layover for two weeks, and you didn't mention you had a sister."

"I had dinner with Tina on that trip back here, but it wasn't high on my mind that night."

"You weren't wearing a ring."

"You weren't, either, but you had worn one at one

time. The skin on that finger was lighter. It had been a wide gold band."

Kaitlyn suddenly pushed her dish away. "I think we should stop with the questions now. If you want to get the crib put together, now's probably a good time. I can watch Erica if she wakes up."

"You're running again," he said.

"And you're being too nosy. Just because I came to help you, doesn't mean—"

"It doesn't mean that you'll kiss me," Adam filled in, with a twinkle in his eye. Then he pushed his plate away, too. "You're right. I'd better take advantage of the quiet time and get that crib put together. We can only hope that someone with a Ph.D. can figure it out."

Thirty minutes later, the crib was assembled. Adam had seemed skilled at putting it together even though he'd never done it before. Kaitlyn helped by fitting the sheet onto the mattress. Then Adam laid Erica on it.

"Are we sure she's okay?" Adam asked her.

"She's just as worn-out as you are."

"If she sleeps this much now, she's going to be awake at midnight, isn't she?"

Kaitlyn gave a small laugh. "Now you're catching on."

"I'm a quick study. I'll have to make sure I set more than one alarm at intervals so I wake up to check on her. Maybe I should buy one of those baby monitors the next time I go shopping."

"Are you going to wheel her into the bedroom?"

They both looked in that direction and then at each other.

"Would you like to see how I don't have it decorated?" he asked, with his brows lifting and lowering.

She laughed. "Not unless you need help pushing the crib in."

He shook his head. "No, I'll crash on the sofa tonight. I want to be near the bottles and formula, the diapers and anything else she'll need."

He was putting the baby's comfort before his, and Kaitlyn admired that. She thought again about her responsibilities with The Mommy Club—her responsibility to make sure Erica got the care she needed, and Adam got the help he needed. That his sister did, too, for that matter. Families were what The Mommy Club was all about.

She had office hours tomorrow morning and a meeting at the hospital in the afternoon. She'd already be in Sacramento. The question was—did she want to get more involved or didn't she? Adam could still have a rough night with the baby and that wouldn't make tomorrow any easier for him.

"I'm going to try to call Tina again," he said. "It's almost nine. Maybe she'll pick up."

"You think her guard will be down because it's later in the day?"

"Maybe." He took his phone from his belt and left another message for his sister.

That call, and the expression on Adam's face—as if bracing for a storm—had Kaitlyn say, "If you'd like, I'll go with you to Tina's apartment tomorrow."

He came around the side of the crib to where she was standing. "You want to see where Tina lives in case she comes back?"

"That's partly my reason."

He was closer now, towering above her, sex appeal oozing from him. "What's the other part?"

"It's not as if you're a complete stranger, Adam. I care about what happens to you."

"Well, *that's* an admission. Did you think about me this past year?"

Oh, no. She wasn't going to admit that. "I really should be going, and you should catch a nap if you can while Erica is still sleeping. You might need it later."

He narrowed his eyes and studied her. "You know, when Jase first introduced me to you, you seemed cool and hid behind a polite reserve. But once we started talking and laughing and joking, Kaitlyn, I saw what was underneath it, and you know I did."

"You're not what you seem to be, either, Adam. I looked you up on Google. I found photos of you with beautiful women on your arm at community and charity functions. I knew about that track scholarship to UC Davis. But I also discovered you were in an accident when you were in college and you were charged with reckless driving. The girl in the car with you was pretty seriously hurt. The custom-made suit and the boy-next-door flirting hid all that."

She thought Adam might defend himself, that he might tell her what had happened because she knew as well as anyone there was never just one side. But he didn't. His jaw tightened, the nerve in it worked and he stayed silent.

Finally, he broke the stalemate. "So that's why you don't think I'm fit to take care of Erica."

"I want to make sure your care is the right care."

"And if you don't think it is, you'll call in someone more official."

She was a doctor. She'd have no choice.

"Fine," he snapped. "Do you want to meet me there or do you want me to pick you up?"

She retrieved her purse. "I have office hours in the morning and a meeting at the hospital in Sacramento in the afternoon, so I can meet you at your sister's apartment around three if you give me the address."

Without a comment, he went to the table by the sofa where a cordless phone sat along with a pad of paper. He jotted down an address and tore the paper from the pad with a swift jerking movement that told Kaitlyn he was angry. He handed it to her.

Kaitlyn went to the door but he didn't follow her. He stood at Erica's crib looking down at her.

Kaitlyn let herself out.

Chapter Four

The tension between Adam and Kaitlyn was obvious as he carried Erica's car seat into Tina's apartment in Sacramento and Kaitlyn followed. He didn't know why her opinion of him mattered, but it did. Glancing at her, he thought about their conversation before she'd left last night. He'd almost explained exactly what had happened that night when he'd been twenty-one, stupid and in love. However, he considered the possibility that Kaitlyn might not even believe him.

He'd shaken off the bad-boy rep after one of his science profs had truly captured his attention. He'd become interested in earning a graduate degree in something that mattered and a life that could take him away from Fawn Grove, from a broken family, from an accident that had changed *his* life more than his girlfriend's. Sherry hadn't hesitated one instant when he'd stepped up and said *he'd* been driving. A career in law had been her sole goal. That's why he'd accepted the blame. So she wouldn't lose her dream.

Adam had paid a fine, done community service and worked hard to make sure every hospital bill was paid, missing a semester of college. His father had made sure Sherry had received the best care. She'd come out of the whole thing without a spleen, with a broken leg and the aftereffects of a concussion.

Before the police and paramedics arrived, she'd promised Adam she'd never drink and drive again. He knew he'd never let anyone drink and drive again if he could help it. But the whole true story had never come out. He'd taken the blame. His reputation hadn't been a big deal. Hers had.

But telling all that to Kaitlyn…

It just seemed a waste.

He set Erica's carrier on the kitchen table in Tina's cramped apartment as they looked around. This apartment didn't look much different than his condo had yesterday. There was a pile of laundry on the sofa that looked clean, one next to it that looked dirty. Dishes and mugs were strewn about as well as a few baby bottles. There was one bedroom and he and Kaitlyn both peeked into it, their shoulders brushing.

Kaitlyn's gaze met his, and he thought he saw regret there. Regret that she'd told him she knew his background?

He moved back toward his niece.

"This looks as if she left impulsively," Kaitlyn said.

He understood why she'd say that. The bed was unmade. Tina's clothes were scattered here and there along with more of the baby's. There wasn't an inch of the apartment that didn't look like bedlam. The way the inside of Tina's mind was working?

"This isn't her. She's not like this. Tina's as neat as a pin. I used to kid her, because even when she was little, she kept her clothes color-coordinated in her closet. When she came to see me at college, she packed her suitcase the same way."

"Adam, you've experienced firsthand how a baby can turn your life upside down. That obviously happened to Tina. One day she had a life without a child. The next day, she was a mom with twenty-four-hour responsibility…a lifelong responsibility. That can be scary and earth-shattering, and altogether overwhelming."

When Adam didn't respond, she asked, "What does Tina do? For work, I mean."

"She's a paralegal. She told me her boss was giving her three months maternity leave. Apparently she had enough money saved between what Jade left her and my father's gifts."

"So she has to find day care she can trust."

"Yes."

"Do you know if she has a best friend, if she's friends with anyone at work?"

"When she graduated and got this job, she mentioned it was a small law firm and everyone else was older. I think she lost contact with most of her high school friends. Many of them went on to four-year colleges."

"Has she lived here since her mother died?"

"She and Jade shared an apartment. My dad subsidized it until Tina got a job, then she insisted she wanted to be on her own. She wouldn't take my help, either. She's a responsible young adult, Kaitlyn. That's why none of this makes any sense."

Kaitlyn gently touched his arm. He felt that touch in every fiber of his being.

"It does make sense," she explained. "In a world of hormones and after-pregnancy feelings. But she has to want help for you to be able to give it."

"Or for The Mommy Club to give it," he muttered. "Can you watch Erica for a few minutes while I search through Tina's desk in her bedroom? Maybe I can find a clue as to where she's gone."

"Sure, I can. Or if you need help, I can just bring her in."

"I've got this," he said with that determined note Kaitlyn recognized. He didn't want to need anyone else.

She wandered about Tina's apartment, very different from Adam's. There were lots of pictures standing about, mostly of Tina and of a woman who Kaitlyn guessed was her mom. There were also photos of Tina and a younger Adam, photos of Tina and Adam with a man whom Kaitlyn assumed might be his father and Tina's stepfather.

There was already a photo of a newborn Erica propped beside the TV. Some hospitals provided those photos, but Tina had gone to the trouble of framing it and setting it in a prominent place. Not something an uncaring mom would do.

When Erica began fussing a little, Kaitlyn scooped her from the pink leopard lining of the car seat and carried her into the kitchen. She couldn't resist holding a baby. Doing it was always bittersweet. Yet she looked forward to the day when she might have her own child in her arms.

On the refrigerator, she spotted magnets for take-out food services, but not much else. Feeling helpless, Kaitlyn returned Erica to her car seat, gave her arm a tender stroke and then started straightening up. At least that was something she could do.

When Adam returned to the living room, he noticed right away. "You didn't have to do that."

"I know. Did you find anything?"

"No, just some work-related notes with her laptop. She's planning to return to work November 1."

"If she's making plans, that's a good sign."

"Those plans obviously changed."

Adam's look was pensive, and Kaitlyn knew he was thinking plenty of thoughts he wasn't sharing with her.

"What are you thinking about doing?" she asked cautiously.

He looked over at Erica, around the apartment and then back at Kaitlyn. "I'm thinking about calling a private investigator."

That was well and good, but there could be repercussions. "How do you think Tina will feel if she knows you put a private investigator on her trail?"

"She'll know I care…that I want to find her."

"She'll also know you didn't trust her to come back on her own."

"Whose side are you on? You insinuated she might not want to come back."

"And if she doesn't want to come back, and you drag her back, what will happen then?" Kaitlyn asked.

"I don't know, but at least I'll be able to talk to her."

"And convince her to do what you want her to do?"

"Erica needs her mother and I need—"

"To be free of all of it?" Kaitlyn filled in.

"You *do* think the worst of me, don't you? No, I don't want to be free of all of it. I want to be sure Tina and Erica are having a good life."

"What happens in a month if nothing is settled, and you still don't know where Tina is?"

She thought he might get angry, might even blow his top. Maybe she was testing him to see exactly how he would react.

Instead of becoming angry at her questions, he crossed to Erica and looked down at her as if all he wanted to do was protect her. "I'll work out something. I always do."

She wasn't exactly sure what that meant, but she didn't have time to question him further because her phone buzzed. When she saw the number, she said, "It's Sara Cramer—Jase's wife. Do you mind if I take this?"

He shrugged. "Go ahead. I'll wash up the dishes."

Kaitlyn answered the call. "Hi, Sara. How are you?"

"I'm fine. Did you finish with your meeting?"

"I did, and now I'm…" She hesitated. "I'm in the middle of a situation."

"For The Mommy Club?"

"Yes."

"But you can't talk about it."

"Right."

"Oh, somebody's with you. I won't hold you up. I just wondered if you could stop out at the winery. I need to go over a few things with you for the bachelor auction. Marissa's planning the setup, of course—table linens and decorations. She's so good at planning events. But the truth is, I need more bachelors. Besides the bachelor auction, I also want to talk to you about the trip that Jase and Amy and I will be taking to Alabama. It's for literacy's sake, that's true, but we might come across some medical situations. I thought maybe you could write me a checklist of things to look for with the kids."

"That's probably a good idea. I'd be glad to do that."

Kaitlyn glanced into the kitchen at Adam, and she had an idea. "Is Jase going to be there within the next couple of hours?"

"I think so. He's making sure all the renovations are finished, and everything's shipshape for when his dad returns home from his European winery trip."

"I might bring along a friend who knows Jase. Is that okay?"

"That's fine. Come whenever you can. We'll be here."

After Kaitlyn ended the call, she went into the kitchen and stood beside Adam, who was rinsing dishes and setting them on a towel.

"How would you like to take a field trip on the way back to the condo?"

He glanced toward his niece. "I don't know how long she's going to sleep."

"I know. But I'm going to stop at Raintree Winery, and I thought you might like to visit, too. I don't think Sara will mind having a baby around, and you can reconnect with Jase."

"Are you thinking I have cabin fever?"

"It's just a suggestion," she said mildly, knowing it would probably be far better if she went to Raintree alone and Adam went home. Just standing here with him, she could feel such a pull toward him. His aftershave was an enticing reason to breathe in. His green eyes seemed to see into places she wanted to keep secret.

When he took a step closer to her, he admitted, "And it was a sound suggestion. When I'm working, I have a good relationship with the guys on my team. When I'm back here, I miss that camaraderie. It would be great to see Jase again."

"Not many women on your teams?"

"A few, but usually, it's all guys. I'd like to see our schools encourage girls to pursue science more vigorously, not just in geology, but in chemistry and biology. Women think differently than men."

"Doesn't that create controversy?"

"It can, but instead of controversy, the new ideas can often complement each other. It's the way science advances. You know that."

Yes, she did. "So education is important to you?"

"I guest lecture now and then. In fact, I'll be giving a lecture soon at Wilson University here in Sacramento."

"So you're a professor, too."

"As I said, a man of all trades."

"Many talents," she murmured, his exact words.

"Many, many talents," he assured her, bending closer.

She should move away; she really should. But if she did, he'd say she was running again. So she didn't run...she stood her ground. But she braced her hands on his chest. "Adam, I can't."

"It's not as if I didn't expect that," he said a little wryly. "But you can't blame a guy for trying."

"Trying to do what?"

"Damned if I know. Maybe I'm just trying to convince you that the chemistry we felt that night didn't end there."

She couldn't break eye contact. "Why does it matter?"

His brows arched. "Because you seem dead set on denying anything happened. Are you avoiding the effects of chemistry?"

"I know the consequences."

"Believe me, so do I."

"Because of what happened when you were twenty-one?" she guessed.

He ran his hand through his hair and shook his head. "You don't want to go there."

"No, *you* don't want to go there."

He took a step away from her and crossed his arms over his chest. "You already know what happened."

"I know what was reported."

He cocked his head. "There's no need to go into it further."

For some reason, she felt he was hiding something. What could he possibly be hiding? His reputation had been tarnished that night, and he'd probably worked since then to change it. He seemed to be that kind of man. But there was a reason he wouldn't discuss it, and that made her even more curious about him.

"What are you going to do about Tina?"

"I found an address book in her desk. She must have kept it from when she was little. I'm going to contact the names in there and find out if she's contacted anybody."

A little cry came from Erica, and they both went into the living room to check on her.

"That new formula seems to agree with her," he said.

"If she couldn't digest the other one, she was uncomfortable every time she ate. No wonder she fussed."

She checked Erica's diaper. "She really should be changed. If you want to start making some of those calls, I'd be glad to do it."

"She's my responsibility," he said, ready to take over again if he had to.

"I know." She waited for him to make a decision.

"I feel as if I should be paying you for your time," he said gruffly.

"My Mommy Club work is all volunteer."

"I don't like to owe anyone."

"You don't owe me anything, Adam."

"I'm going to owe you at least one very expensive dinner when this is all done."

After a last look at Erica, he picked up the address book on the table. "I'll make those calls, then we can see if returning to Raintree Winery brings back memories for both of us."

Before she could comment on *that* idea, he took the address book and his phone to his sister's bedroom for privacy.

Kaitlyn couldn't decide if she wanted to remember that night at the winery, or if she didn't. Returning to Raintree Winery with Adam was certain to resurrect something other than thoughts of wine tasting.

As Kaitlyn followed Adam's SUV onto the Raintree Winery property, she thought, not for the first time, that she'd never seen a more serene or beautiful setting. Besides the acres of vineyards with trellises, there were gardens blooming with roses, marigolds and chrysanthemums.

They parked behind the main house across from the guest cottage. No sooner had they exited their cars, than Sara and Jase were there, all smiles, welcoming them into their home.

Seeing Erica, Sara scooped her up into her arms. "She's a cutie. Do you think she'll like sitting in the garden?"

"We can try it," Adam said. "On her new formula, she's been sleeping and seems more contented. But you never know when she's going to get unhappy with the world."

Sara laughed. "That's the fun of babies."

The look Sara exchanged with her husband told Kaitlyn volumes. There might be some baby fun at the winery very soon.

Amy came running over to her mom and looked up at Erica. "Can I play with her?"

"She's not quite as big as Jordan, and I don't think she's ready for your kind of play. But she might like one of your stuffed animals. Why don't you go get one."

Amy grinned at her mom and ran into the house.

They all went to a covered seating area. "How about a glass of wine?" Jase asked.

Kaitlyn glanced at Adam, and they remembered the last time they had sampled the wine.

Adam said, "Nothing for me."

Kaitlyn added, "We know your wines are great, but

Adam hasn't had much sleep, and I never know when I'll get a call. But something cold would be good."

Jase gave Sara an indulgent look. "Since your arms are full, I'll get iced tea."

Sara glanced up at Adam. "So this is your niece."

"Yes, she is. I'm watching her for my sister."

Kaitlyn knew Adam didn't want to go further than that, and Sara seemed to get that signal. Erica made a little noise and Sara rocked her naturally, knowing exactly what to do.

She said to Kaitlyn, "Jase tells me the letter you wrote for his column in the paper will be published next week. How do you feel about that?"

Kaitlyn turned to Adam to explain. "Jase is spotlighting members of The Mommy Club and their stories. I told him I'd like to write an open letter to the women of Fawn Grove instead of doing the interview. He liked it and thinks it's a good idea."

"His series is the reason I called The Mommy Club," Adam revealed to Sara.

"I was hesitant for *my* interview to go public," Sara explained. "The series is online, too, so people can make comments. You never know what they're going to say. It can be unsettling."

"I don't think Kaitlyn gets unsettled often," Adam responded.

Not unless you kiss me, she thought.

Now just where had that come from? Sitting next to him was enough to ruffle her for the whole day.

"The Mommy Club's having a fund-raiser next Friday," Sara told him.

"Really? I'd be glad to make a donation."

Sara gave Adam a quick once-over and Kaitlyn

shrugged, knowing what she was thinking. Adam would make a terrific "bachelor" for the auction.

Sara opened with, "Jase said you are the kind of guy who likes to have a good time."

Adam's expression grew cautious. "I suppose I do."

"I mean, you're no stranger to a tuxedo, right?"

"I've worn one now and then." His voice became even more wary.

As well it should, Kaitlyn thought.

"Let me tell you our problem, and then you let me know if you want to help."

"Fair enough."

"We're having a bachelor auction."

Adam's brows drew together. "Uh-oh."

Sara laughed and Kaitlyn had to smile herself. Yes it was definitely an uh-oh moment, but Sara could convince almost anyone to do anything.

"It's like this," her friend admitted. "We had enough bachelors, we really did. But two of the businessmen had trips coming up."

"I'll just bet those trips were absolutely necessary," Adam said.

"They were," Sara protested, humor in her voice. "And another of our bachelors is sick, really sick. He had bronchitis and then pneumonia. So we're short. Now our chief winemaker, Liam, has finally agreed to do it. But we really need at least one other guy, so we can round it out to an even dozen. This money is important, Adam. The Mommy Club does have a benefactress, but we can't rely strictly on her forever."

"You don't have to convince me that this is a good cause. It is," he agreed. "But the idea of walking down a runway…"

Sara waved her hand in front of his face.

"Oh, no, don't worry about that. It's not like you see on the TV shows. We're going to have the auction in our events room. It's just going to be some fake stairs you walk up and then down. Maybe you stop at the top for a couple of minutes. But that's it. And wouldn't you love to have an exciting date with somebody new?"

"Right now, my life's filled with enough newness. And besides all that, I wouldn't have anybody to baby-sit Erica."

Some imp Kaitlyn didn't know she possessed urged her to say, "I'll babysit if someone buys you. I'd be glad to do it. That will be my donation. Well, at least part of it."

At that moment, Jase came back with a tray of iced tea glasses and a plate of sweet rolls made with the winery's own grape jelly. Amy's grin spread ear to ear.

"Have they talked you into it yet?" Jase asked.

"You knew your wife was going to try to do that?"

"I knew my wife and Kaitlyn were probably going to tag team you. Why don't we take a walk and let them discuss a new strategy. I'll show you our vines."

"Sounds good."

Kaitlyn wondered if Adam would even consider being part of the bachelor auction. After all, how would she feel if another woman went out on a date with him? She shouldn't have any feelings about it at all.

Not at all.

Jase and Adam walked in silence toward the Merlot vineyard, just enjoying the scent of the fall earth and the beautiful dark blue berries on the trellises.

Mountains rose up in the distance. Raintree Winery was indeed a special place. Adam could almost understand why Jase had settled here.

As they turned away from the main buildings and the house, Adam asked, "Do you miss your old life— flying the world, shooting pictures no one else can get?"

Adam knew Jase had won a Pulitzer before he'd gotten shot by bandits in Africa. He'd come back to Raintree to recuperate. That's when he'd met Sara for the first time, when she was his physical therapist. Two years later, when her house burned down, he gave her a place to stay at the guest cottage. A widow then, that kindness was all it had taken to bring them back together again. Anyone could tell when they looked at each other that they were in love.

In love. Exactly what was that? Adam wasn't sure he'd know it if it landed on his head.

Jase plucked a grape off the vine and handed it to Adam. "Smell it, squeeze it open and taste it. This is where winemaking starts. I learned the ins and outs of it when I was a teenager. It was the one thing my dad and I connected on. When I returned from Africa, this land, these grapes and finally Sara, made staying more important than leaving, made wanting a real family a goal. It's not as if I'm tethered here. Sara and Amy both will be traveling to Alabama with me for a literacy campaign. And I'm thinking about something else for the new year."

"That just involves you?"

"It could, but I'd rather make it a family jaunt. Sara would like to study some methods of physical therapy in Switzerland, and I'd like to get a take on parenthood there. We could blog as we go, or I could try to sell the series with my contacts. It's just in its idea stage."

"But it sounds like a way to stay involved in journalism. And I imagine when you go away, now you look forward to coming home."

"I hadn't thought about it like that, but I guess it's true. What about you?"

"What about me?"

"When we met in Africa, you said you were out of the U.S. more than you were in it."

Adam had told Kaitlyn the same thing.

"So is it the traveling that excites you…or the work?" Jase asked.

"It's the work that fascinates me, not the traveling. I think that's a realization I've been coming to over the past few years. My last trip really brought it home. I have a commitment in a few weeks in Thailand, but if everything isn't resolved with my sister, I can't imagine leaving. Do you enjoy being a dad?"

Jase grinned. "I haven't been one very long. But when Amy looks at me with those big eyes and asks me a question that she expects me to know the answer to, I feel ten feet tall. Tea parties? That's another matter."

Adam chuckled. "You've always related well to kids. That's easy to see from all those photographs you took in the refugee camps. They looked at you as if you could do no wrong."

"So what's it like caring for a baby when you've never cared for a baby?" Jase wanted to know.

"It's damn hard. I haven't really slept since she arrived. I mean, even when she sleeps, I worry about her not sleeping. I worry she's going to wake up and need something. With every little sound, I'm practically on my feet, ready to pick up a bottle or a diaper or something."

It was obvious Jase was trying not to laugh. "My guess is that's a new-parent reaction."

"But I'm not a new parent. And when all this is over—" He blew out a large breath. "I'm just hoping The Mommy Club can give Tina the help she needs."

"They're an excellent group. They know how to delegate and they have lots of branches, from the thrift store to food drives to babysitting services to day care. It will work out, Adam, but it might take time."

Time.

Wasn't that a precious commodity?

He and Jase talked about other things then—the political situation in Africa, the famine in Ethiopia, how bringing water to some areas would mean the difference between life and death. They ended up talking about the winery and new wines that were up for awards. Adam found himself relaxing as he hadn't in a long time, even before Erica had arrived in his care.

After they returned to the garden, Amy was sitting beside Erica, playing with her toes. Kaitlyn was looking down at them with an odd expression on her face. It looked to Adam like…regret. He suddenly wanted to know her story very badly.

When the women saw the men, they looked up hopefully.

"Did you make a decision?" Kaitlyn asked, and he knew she fully expected him to say no.

To his surprise, what came out of his mouth was something else entirely. "All right. I volunteer to be one of your bachelors on one condition."

"What?" Sara asked cautiously.

"You let me go first, second or third so I can get it over with."

Everyone laughed, and Kaitlyn studied Adam with renewed admiration. He really was a good sport. *He really is a good kisser, too,* that little imp inside of her reminded her. All at once, she thought about what another kiss would be like. All at once, she could imagine his lips on hers, his hands—

"Kaitlyn?"

She'd missed a question.

"I'm sorry. My mind was wandering."

At Adam's glance, her cheeks flushed because she had the suspicion he knew where it had wandered.

"If Adam gets bought, *can* he count on you to baby-sit?" Sara asked again.

"Of course I can," Adam said. "Kaitlyn's the kind of person you can count on."

Kaitlyn thought about the last thing her husband had ever said to her. "I counted on you to put us first and you didn't. That's what caused the end of our marriage."

She still didn't have it all sorted out properly. Until she did, she couldn't think about getting involved with another man.

However, she wasn't going to get involved with Adam. She was just going to babysit for him.

Chapter Five

Adam's time with Kaitlyn visiting at Raintree had been enjoyable. To his chagrin, he didn't want that time with her to end. Back in Fawn Grove, she'd be going her way and he'd be going his.

As he drove toward town, he considered the bachelor auction he'd volunteered for. Sara had told him the list of bachelors would be circulated far and wide along with their photos. Their bios would be listed in ads from Sacramento to Stockton. He hadn't protested. After all, the event was for a good cause. He glanced back at Erica through the rearview mirror. A drive always seemed to lull her into a peaceful sleep. He didn't know what that meant for sleep tonight, but he was definitely in the go-with-the-flow plan right now. Checking his rearview mirror again, he saw Kaitlyn's car behind his.

Impulsively, he pressed a button on the dashboard and said, "Call Kaitlyn."

Seconds later, Kaitlyn answered, "Yes, Adam?"

"There's an ice-cream stand about a quarter mile down this road. Let's pull over."

"It's almost dinnertime," she said with some amusement.

"We can get walnuts on a sundae for protein. Come on."

"I really should get going—"

"You're running again."

Her silence met his statement. He wanted to know more about her before her background went public. He had the feeling it was something she hadn't shared easily up until now, and he didn't want to read about it in the newspaper or online. He wanted to get to know her better. But he wasn't going to spook her by telling her that. Not yet.

Taking a lighter tone, he coaxed, "Ice-cream sundaes with hot fudge, whipped cream, a cherry on the top."

She laughed. "Okay. It's such a beautiful evening, I don't want to go in yet, either. I'll meet you there."

Minutes later, he pulled into the parking area beside the small ice-cream stand. Kaitlyn could easily drive on by. But she didn't. Her sedan pulled in beside his SUV.

There were only a few cars, and one person ordering ice cream at the window. Picnic tables dotted the back of the property near live oaks and some alders that gave shade. He climbed out of his SUV and unstrapped Erica's car seat. As he carried it toward one of the picnic tables, Kaitlyn followed him.

He set it on the table and said, "She looks like a pink angel."

Kaitlyn stood very close beside him and he would have liked to have dropped his arm around her shoulders. He would have liked to kiss her. When she looked up at him, he almost did. But a kiss could send her running for the hills.

"Do you want to watch her while I get the sundaes, or do you want to get the sundaes?"

"I'll watch her," she said, her voice all soft and tender as any woman's would be who loved children.

"So is it hot fudge, or something else?"

"I'm going to be really decadent. Hot fudge over raspberry ice cream, a dab of whipped cream on top, no nuts, no cherry."

"A woman with particular tastes."

"What are *you* getting?" she asked.

"A double-decker sundae with an extra layer of hot fudge, extra walnuts, whipped cream and a cherry on the top."

"A man with extravagant tastes," she quipped.

He laughed and went to buy their ice-cream sundaes.

When he returned to the table, he set their sundaes in front of each of them. He sat close to her, their elbows touching, and she didn't move away. Neither did he. Progress.

They ate in silence for a couple of minutes until she said, "We backed you into a corner with that bachelor auction. If you really don't want to do it, you can back out."

"I don't back out once I commit."

His words must have surprised her—her gaze rose to his.

"You might not believe it," he said, "but even when I was a teenager, I was reliable. I tried to be for Tina. She'd had so much uncertainty in her life. I wanted her to be able to count on me."

"But you went to college and couldn't be there for her."

"Long distance doesn't mean out of mind, and I let her know that. When she came up to school to spend time with me, I made sure my calendar was clear. It's always been that way." He paused. "But I don't want to talk anymore about me and Tina."

He studied Kaitlyn as she swirled ice cream with her spoon, as she lifted it to her mouth, as she ate it and savored it. He practically groaned. He wanted her for the most basic reasons, and every little thing she did made his blood race faster.

He must not have hidden his desire as well as he should have, because her breath caught a little when their eyes met. Her hand stilled. Ice cream dripped from her spoon into the dish.

They seemed frozen in a little world of their own where remembering could get them into big trouble. He leaned closer to her, put his arm around her, let his jaw rub down the side of her face. She didn't jerk away or tell him not to do it, so he did it again. He didn't think she was wearing perfume, but there was a sweet scent around her tied-back hair that carried just as much potency.

His lips trailed down her temple to her ear and he whispered, "I want to kiss you, but I want to get to know you better even more."

He leaned away, but kept his connection to her with his eyes. "Tell me what's going to come out in the paper next week."

Her eyes widened and she looked surprised, maybe even shocked. "Adam."

"If it's going to be public, why not tell me now?"

"It's a personal story. Writing it down was therapeutic and I knew it would help others. Telling you face-to-face seems—"

"Too intimate? As intimate as kissing? As intimate as shedding our clothes?"

Her shoulders stiffened and she shifted away. "All right, you've made your point. Maybe undressing physically is a lot easier than undressing emotionally."

This time he covered her hand with his and held on. He didn't say any more.

Kaitlyn glanced at their hands, and he felt her release a resigned sigh. "Tom and I met when I was an intern. We got married later in my residency. He had a career in advertising and marketing for the wine industry. I decided to become part of the Fawn Grove practice, and we moved here though he preferred Sacramento. After we did, I got pregnant."

Pregnant. Kaitlyn had been pregnant. He had a foreboding of what was coming because he'd glimpsed the sadness in her eyes when she held Erica. It was mixed in with other emotions, but it was there.

He squeezed her hand. "What happened?"

"Somehow, preeclampsia sneaked up on me."

At Adam's blank look, she explained, "It's a condition that happens to some pregnant women. They start retaining fluid, their blood pressure spikes. Of course, I knew all the signs. But I'd been working

long hours for years. I was used to pushing myself
to my limits, physically and every other way. When I
was pregnant, I got regular checkups, I watched what
I ate, I stopped caffeine. That had kept me going a
lot of the time, even though I didn't want to admit it.
But I had this case in PEDS—a premature baby who
needed a couple of procedures. I don't know if I was
too focused on that—"

She shook her head. "I'll never know. But the preeclampsia caused a miscarriage when I was six months
pregnant. A few months later, my marriage fell apart.
I didn't really get back on my feet until I joined The
Mommy Club support group. That's what helped me
overcome it all. That group helped me see that I wasn't
to blame for everything."

"Of course you weren't to blame for everything,"
Adam said gruffly. "I'm not a medical professional
but even *I* know that. Stuff happens."

He said it with such wry resignation that Kaitlyn
looked at him with appreciation. "Thank you," she
murmured.

"For what?" he asked. "For knowing you're human
just like everyone else? I've got to admit, sometimes
your composure is a little unshakable, and that can
be scary."

"Composure is just a way to try to keep in control."

"When you're feeling out of control?"

"Uh-oh. I think I've given away a secret."

Adam shook his head. "I won't hold it against you."
Then he asked, "So why did your marriage come
apart?"

"Isn't that obvious?"

"No, actually it's not. A tragedy like that sometimes brings people together."

"Not in our case. Tom blamed me. I was a doctor. I should have seen what was happening. I should have known."

Without thinking, Adam slipped his arm around Kaitlyn's shoulders. "That was your ex-husband's inadequacies talking."

She shook her head. "I believed him. I think that's what destroyed our marriage. I let him blame me."

"And where was he in all this? Was he watching your physical condition? Was he giving you foot rubs at night? Was he close enough to see any changes?"

Adam easily saw the pain in Kaitlyn's eyes when she shook her head. "We were up-and-coming professionals with careers. He wants to own his own advertising and marketing company someday."

Adam would have asked more questions and held her even tighter, but at that moment his cell phone beeped.

Kaitlyn glanced at his belt as he released her and went for the phone.

"It's Tina," he said, snatching it and holding it to his ear. As soon as he clicked it on, he heard silence. "Tina?"

Her end of the line went dead.

He swore and speed-dialed her number but she didn't answer.

"What am I supposed to make of that?" he asked the universe in general.

"Maybe she wants to let you know she's okay."

"That's a funny way of doing it. If we don't talk, I

can't tell her I care. I can't tell her there's help if she needs it."

Looking thoughtful, Kaitlyn pushed her ice-cream dish away. "Maybe you *can* tell her. Maybe what Tina really wants is to make sure Erica's okay."

"I can leave daily messages on her phone as progress reports. That might work."

"At least she'd know how Erica's doing, and what you're doing for her. You can tell her the cute things."

Adam studied baby Erica who was still sleeping peacefully. "I can send her pictures, too."

"A picture *is* worth a thousand words."

He snapped a picture of Erica with his phone. Then he typed in a line about going for ice cream and enjoying the summer night.

To Kaitlyn he said, "I'll leave a voice message for her later. I don't want to bombard her, or make her sorry she tried to call."

Kaitlyn nodded as if she understood every bit of it, and maybe she did.

His phone back on his belt, Adam dropped his arm around Kaitlyn's shoulders again and turned her toward him. "Thank you for telling me about your exhusband and your miscarriage. I know it's not easy to share memories that still cause pain."

"The pain turns into regret more than anything," Kaitlyn said.

She was right about that. Maybe he and Kaitlyn were more alike than they were different. He didn't know. He just knew he was monumentally attracted to her, physically and otherwise. But right now, the physical was taking precedence.

Taking her chin in his hand, he tipped her face up

to him. She was watching him with such expectancy that he didn't think twice about lowering his head. He didn't think twice about covering her lips with his.

The alders and oaks sheltered them. The falling dusk enveloped them. The quiet seemed to intensify everything about the kiss. Adam wanted more. When his tongue slid into Kaitlyn's mouth, he knew that she did, too. She gripped his shoulders tighter. She gave a soft moan. She tasted him back and that was the most exciting sensation of all.

She was everything he'd remembered and dreamed of in his long nights away, when that winery office and that night were across the world.

Kaitlyn was the one to break the kiss. She was the one to stop them before it went deeper. He wasn't surprised. After all, she'd ended the passion once before. Now he could understand why a little better.

She wasn't the type of woman who usually had affairs. She was dedicated and loyal—the marrying kind. Maybe he'd known that from the beginning and that's why he hadn't contacted her since they'd first met. He was loyal, but he definitely wasn't the marrying kind.

"Wrong place, wrong time again," he joked huskily, watching for her reaction.

"I'm not sure there will be a right place and the right time," she confessed.

"Because of you, or because of me?" He was suddenly a little angry at that assumption.

"Adam, I don't—"

"Sleep around?" he filled in. "Yeah, I figured that out. Sometimes, Kaitlyn, grabbing the moment can be as worthwhile as looking for a future."

"Spoken like a man with no roots," she said lightly, but for some reason her words unsettled him a lot.

"And what are *your* roots?"

She looked surprised that he even asked. "The Mommy Club, friends, my profession."

"*Roots,* Kaitlyn. You do for The Mommy Club. You do for your practice. You probably do for your friends, too."

"I don't know what you're getting at."

"I think we're both rootless."

"You're wrong."

"It wouldn't be the first time, but you have just as many walls as I do. Maybe a little sex could break them down."

She looked outraged. "Maybe a little sex could get us into a whole lot of trouble. My heart isn't detached from passion and desire. Is yours?"

"I don't analyze it."

"Maybe you should."

He'd put her on the defensive, and he hadn't intended to do that. When he reached out to touch her, she backed away, and he could have predicted the next words out of her mouth.

She said, "I've got to go."

He nodded. Kaitlyn had become a woman on the go so she didn't have to feel. She could feel for her little patients and she could feel for moms who needed help. But he wondered how much she could feel for herself. In many ways, he was the same.

Sweeping up the trash, he dumped it into the can close by. Then he went to Erica, picked up her car seat and walked Kaitlyn to her car.

As she slid in, he said, "If The Mommy Club has

a list of possible babysitters, I'd appreciate it. I have to get some work done in preparation for my trip to Thailand. I also have that guest lecture spot coming up. I'd like to interview and check references of anybody I might use to take care of Erica."

"Of course," Kaitlyn said with a nod. "I'll see that you get the list."

"So you're not going to call a social worker in on the case?"

"At this time, I don't think that's necessary."

She was being polite and so was he.

So be it.

By the time he took Erica to his car and tucked her safely inside, Kaitlyn had driven away.

Erica's cries always tore at Adam's heart. The following afternoon, he tried to tell himself babies cried to communicate with their world. At least in part.

After he scooped her into his arms from her crib, he picked up a bottle on the end table and sat in the armchair. She was still crying as he touched the nipple to her lips. But then she latched on.

As she greedily drank, he wondered what he was having for supper. There was leftover Chinese take-out in the fridge. He should go to the store, but handling Erica and grocery bags didn't seem like a good idea. He was hoping Kaitlyn would call him or email him that list.

He had to admit, he wanted to see Kaitlyn again, and again, and again. He'd never quite felt this way about a woman, and it unnerved him. He looked down at the baby in his arms. Just as Erica unnerved him.

He couldn't believe how he was actually coming to enjoy feeding her, rocking her, watching her fall asleep. He was beginning to wonder what would happen if Tina didn't come back. He wondered what would happen if she didn't want to be a mom. He certainly couldn't let this little girl be put in foster care. On the other hand, did he want to be a dad?

He wasn't sure.

Erica looked up at him with wide blue eyes.

"You know," he said in a conversational tone, "I remember the first day I met your mom. She had pigtails. She was scared that she had to come live somewhere new. Your grandmother Jade told her I was her big brother and I'd keep her safe. I don't even think I knew what *safe* meant back then. I thought it meant watching her so she didn't fall or do any stupid stunts like I'd tried. But I'm not sure that's what she meant at all. I think she meant I should create a bond with her that would last forever. But over the past few years, I think I messed up. I thought your mom was an adult now, and she didn't need me watching over her. But that's not true."

Erica made a little sound, and he took the bottle from her and burped her. That was easier now, too, since Kaitlyn had shown him how to do it.

Adam had just put Erica on his shoulder and was patting her back when his doorbell rang.

He wasn't expecting anyone, unless Tina had decided to come home.

Standing, he rushed to the door and pulled it open. When he saw Kaitlyn, he didn't quite know what to say.

"I hope I didn't disturb you," she began.

"No. No," he said more vigorously. "For an instant there, I thought Tina might be coming home."

Kaitlyn could only imagine the ups and downs of what Adam was experiencing. That was one of the reasons she'd stopped by after hospital rounds. She'd found she couldn't stay away. Every phone call, every ring of the doorbell, and Adam thought Tina could be back home. When she wasn't, that had to be heart-breaking.

"May I come in?" she asked, though she noticed he seemed to be lost in thought. "I have that list for you of babysitters and possibly helpers."

"Sure, come on in. Erica was just telling me she was full."

"Oh, she was?"

If Adam was talking to Erica, that meant he was forming a relationship with her instead of just caring for her. "What else has she been telling you?"

"She definitely doesn't like those booties we got for her. She kicks them off. She prefers the pink socks rather than the yellow ones. She concentrates on them more often. She's definitely not crazy about having her hair washed, what there is of it."

Kaitlyn laughed. "In other words, she's wrapping you around her little finger."

Adam shrugged. "Something like that. I'm going to put her in the crib in the bedroom. Stay put."

She never thought of herself as someone who couldn't face life head-on. But she'd left him abruptly last evening, and she wasn't going to let that happen now. Last night she'd revealed too much. But when he touched her and when he kissed her, she had reactions she'd never had to a man before. Her desire for him threw her totally off balance.

Adam returned to the living room a few minutes later. "She's asleep."

Before he could bring up anything personal, Kaitlyn turned to common ground. Taking a folded piece of paper from her purse, she handed it to him.

"Besides babysitters, there's also info on there about a new-parent workshop that might help you cope."

"I'm coping just fine."

She looked around the living room that was much more organized than the first time she came. "Everyone can use a little help."

He came very close to her. "Tell me, Kaitlyn, what will help *us*?"

She didn't pretend not to understand.

"Have you ever thought about a night with me, with no responsibilities, no agenda and no time restrictions?" he asked.

The idea of a night with Adam stopped her cold. She couldn't even think straight.

"Why didn't you just call this morning? You could have given me this information over the phone or in an email."

Standing this close, she could still feel everything male about him—his scent, his strength, his determination. She said weakly, "I wanted to check on Erica."

He narrowed his eyes and came so close she could feel his breath on her cheek. "Tell the truth."

She only hesitated a moment. "I like you."

He broke into a grin. Then he kissed her—really, really hard. After he broke away and stared into her eyes for a moment, he kissed her again, this time with such coaxing passion, she wrapped her arms around his neck and let her purse fall to the floor.

Chapter Six

Kaitlyn was hardly aware of her purse slipping to the floor. She was aware that her need for Adam seemed to be greater than any need she'd ever experienced.

Her fingers were in his hair. His were in hers. His kiss was fiery and over-the-top hungry, and all she could do was respond to it. Maybe this time she was aware they were somewhere safer than the winery office. Maybe her time with Adam had built such a heat in her body it had to burst out. Maybe some passion was just too big to ignore. Maybe because he seemed to desire her as much as she desired him, maybe because they hadn't stopped thinking about each other for a year, maybe all that played into what happened next.

For once, she didn't think about a month from now. She didn't think about an hour from now. All she could think about was Adam's kiss, her tongue playing with his, the exquisite feel of his touch as his fingers drifted down her neck, slid around her and caressed her back.

She hadn't been touched, really touched, in so long. Each stroke of Adam's fingertips took her deeper into desire that seemed to have no bounds. When Adam sought the hem of her shirt and lifted it up over her head, she didn't care that she was shirtless. She just wanted to make him the same way. His T-shirt was loose around his hips, and she was glad for that. Right now easy was better. Easy was the opposite of what she experienced on a daily basis. Easy meant this was right, didn't it?

They had to stop kissing to take his shirt off, and neither of them seemed to want to. While she fumbled with his, he tried to kiss her neck. She laughed, and it felt so good to laugh in this way, to feel free enough to be naked and not care.

Adam's skin was hot, and she couldn't get enough of touching him. She explored the nubs of his spine, his taut back muscles, and then her hands slid into the back of his jeans. He groaned deep in his throat, and she realized excitement wasn't just a word anymore, not for either of them.

What about Adam turned her on so? His scent? His green eyes that seemed to see right into her? Or was it the strength in his body that seemed to be surrounding her now.

When Adam unfastened her slacks and pushed them and her panties down her legs, any thought left in her head fled.

"Take your shoes off," he encouraged her, as his hands went to his belt buckle, as he unfastened his jeans, kicked off his sneakers, and his clothes fell to the floor, too. When they were both naked, she was in awe of his magnificent body.

Then he ordered, "Hold on to my shoulders." And he knelt down before her.

Hold on to his shoulders? What was he going to—?

She soon figured out his intent as his kiss above her navel sent shivers through her. His tongue dipped lower and her knees almost buckled.

"Hold on to my shoulders," he said again, his voice more husky this time.

"Adam—"

"Don't talk," he advised her. "Just feel."

Feel? How long had it been since she'd let herself feel, let alone feel like this? Tom had never wanted to do what Adam was doing. Tom had never really wanted to know *her*.

Knowing a woman. Knowing a man. Maybe this was what it was all about. Everything Adam was doing was making Kaitlyn feel weak, yet strong at the same time. Weak because the sensations were so exciting. Strong because she realized she had the power to make him *want* to do this.

She held on, not knowing what was going to come next. Adam was an expert lover. As she held on to him, the world spun. Her body wound up tight, tensed then released in a feast of sensation.

He continued to stroke and caress and make sure she knew she wasn't alone. When her orgasm was the strongest, when her climax hit with such ferocity, even holding on to Adam didn't seem to be enough. He helped her collapse against him, but then he laid her back on the carpet, rose above her and entered her with a thrust that caused the sensations to start all over again. He was so masterful it seemed as if he had known that would happen. How could he know? How could he guess? Because he suspected she hadn't been with a man since her husband?

Moments later he found his release and they lay there entwined in each other's arms. They seemed to be experiencing the same euphoria. There was so much pleasure in embracing Adam, having him inside her. She felt fulfilled and complete in some way she hadn't before. He rolled them to their sides with his arms still around her. She floated in the sensual haze of lovemaking.

He leaned away slightly. "It was a long wait, but it was worth it." His grin told her as much as the deep male satisfaction in his voice that he was pleased.

"You couldn't have known you were waiting for me, and certainly you didn't wait to have sex," she said.

His grin faded and his gaze held hers. "I haven't been with a woman since well before the night at the winery."

"But you have a reputation for being one of the most eligible if not elusive bachelors around."

He suddenly looked at her with even more concern. "Maybe, but this elusive, eligible bachelor, who should know better, didn't think about protection."

Kaitlyn felt her face go pale, felt the euphoria slip into the past, felt any number of emotions she didn't want to contemplate. "Oh, my gosh."

That brought a bit of amusement to his eyes. "I take it you're not on the pill?"

"You should have asked me that before we started."

All he had to do was arch a brow.

She shook her head. "No, I'm not blaming you.

I don't know what got into me. I never do anything like this."

"That was obvious a year ago," he agreed.

"How can you be so nonchalant about this?"

"Because there's nothing we can do about it now. All we can do is prepare better the next time."

She rolled away from him and sat up. What *had* she done? Something so out of character she truly felt shell-shocked. "There isn't going to be a next time," she murmured.

Grabbing for her clothes, she quickly slipped on her panties and somehow managed to fasten her bra.

"It sure felt like there'd be a next time."

"Adam, there's no future. You're going to fly off to Thailand!"

He nodded. "Yes, I am, but that project will last about six weeks and then I'll be back."

"So you want to fly in, have sex and then leave again?"

He grinned again. "Sounds like a plan, don't you think?"

She rose to her feet and shook her head. "That's the problem. That's the way you plan. It's not the way *I* plan."

"Tell me again why you came here today, Kaitlyn." He was naked and handsome and built and so blasted sexy.

"I came because I like you," she reminded him. "But at this moment, I don't know if it's true."

He shook his head. "I suppose a woman can change her mind, but you'll like me again, especially after you think about what happened here."

She quickly dressed. "I'm leaving."

"Of course you are. You run when you don't know what else to do."

She never liked it when he brought that up. But now she truly didn't know what else to do. She had to sort it out. She had to hope she wasn't pregnant. She had to hope everything was going to be okay. For her, for Adam, for Erica, for Tina.

Dressed, knowing her hair was probably still mussed, her lips pink from kissing, she picked up her purse and went to the door.

Still sitting there naked, not making a move to dress, Adam called to her, "I'll see you at the bachelor auction on Friday night, right? And you're not going to renege on your offer to babysit while I go out on a date, are you?"

They'd just had sex, and he was talking about going out on a date with another woman. Or was he just teasing her? The amusement in his eyes told her he was. The amusement in his eyes told her he wanted to see her again, and he'd do that one way or another.

She left his condo, more confused than she'd ever been.

On Wednesday morning, as the lone man in a room full of women, Adam definitely felt like a fish out of water. Kaitlyn had given him the information on this new-parent workshop, but she hadn't told him only moms would be here.

"It's you and me, kid," he whispered to Erica, getting used to the feel of her sling against his chest. Though in just over a week, he felt she was growing. She didn't seem to want to put her legs into that sling anymore. She sort of hugged him.

Nah, that was only his imagination. Babies didn't grow that fast, did they? If he were a dad, he'd know these things. If he became a dad…he'd learn them.

No, he wasn't actually thinking about being a dad, was he? But a little voice in his head whispered, *What if Tina doesn't come back? What if you can't find her?* He'd always been a roll-with-the-punches kind of guy. He'd had to be. But in his adult life, he could guess what those next punches were going to be. This situation was totally different.

Giving Erica a little pat, maybe encouragement for them both, he strode into the room a lot more confidently than he felt, straight for the gaggle of women and the little kids who were playing all around them— little babies who were older than Erica, toddlers, maybe even three-year-olds.

An older woman—Adam guessed she might be in her fifties—smiled at him, and her blue eyes said she might understand what he was going through as she extended her hand. "Welcome to our new-parent group. Are you Mr. Preston?"

He recognized her voice. This must be Mary Garcia, the woman he'd contacted from Kaitlyn's list.

"I am."

All of the women standing there gave him a tentative smile and hello. One of them, however, smiled at him boldly and even winked. She extended her hand separate from the others, although she was holding a baby on her hip.

"Carla Jacobs. You're brave, coming into this group. I admire a man who can hold his own in a group of women."

She did, did she? He had a feeling she was a single

mom, no ring on her finger and a come-hither look in her eye. Not what he was looking for.

Mary must have seen that Adam was reluctant to enter into that conversation. "Let's all gather our chairs in a group and talk about what happened this week. Then I want to give strategies for keeping babies happy as well as taking any questions you might have." She glanced at Adam. "And don't be shy. Asking a question is better than not asking a question and having to search for the answer on your own."

Everyone nodded.

He felt absolutely silly carrying the diaper bag Tina had chosen for Erica. It was all pink with blue-and-white-striped piping. But it fit right in with everybody else's diaper bags. So he hooked it on the back of a chair and positioned the chair in the circle with everyone else.

Kaitlyn told herself she was only going to peek in on the group. She was only going to see if Adam had taken her advice and come. Would he be too proud to join such a group? Would he want to sit there in the midst of women? It was always mostly women. Or would that make him uncomfortable?

Okay, so she wanted to know. After what had happened between them, she seemed to want to know everything. The idea she might be carrying his child was unsettling, to say the least. But she wouldn't know for a couple of weeks. If her period was late, she'd use a pregnancy test. A good one.

The room down the hall from her offices was set up for these kinds of meetings. It was meant for teaching workshops and demonstrations and anything that might help parents and kids. She quickly glanced over the group and caught sight of Adam's head. She'd know that thick, vibrant hair anywhere. She'd know the profile of his jaw, the line of his neck, the bend of his shoulders. Yes, indeed, she'd know it anywhere. Sometimes in her dreams she could feel his skin under her fingertips, his heat, and even smell his scent. Absolutely crazy.

She knew the best thing for both of them was for her to stay away from him. She could have someone else check on Erica, have Sara call to see how he was doing, or Marissa, or any number of volunteers. But if he was coming to this workshop, Mary was a good judge of character. She'd be able to tell if Erica was thriving or not.

To Kaitlyn's dismay, before she could exit the room and return to her office to eat a container of yogurt, the group broke up. Chairs were being pushed back. Adam stood and looked toward the door as if he were eager to leave. And, of course—

He spotted her. However, before he could settle Erica from his arms to the sling, before he could reach for the diaper bag, one of the women clasped his arm. Kaitlyn knew Carla because she'd taken care of her little girl, Bonnie, and Carla had freely admitted on more than one occasion that she wanted a dad for her daughter.

As Kaitlyn watched, Carla flirted. Adam bent his head toward her, smiled, rocked Erica a little and held a conversation. Carla was smiling, too, so he couldn't be saying anything she didn't like.

But then this was Adam—the charming bachelor, a man who knew how to give in lovemaking, and had made love to her as if the world were going to end tomorrow.

Maybe that was a slight exaggeration.

He wasn't rushing, or seemingly worried that Kaitlyn might leave. He was smiling again, nodding, shrugging. Kaitlyn was about to go…had actually made her way to the doorway, but she heard Adam call her name, and she stopped. It would be immature to pretend she hadn't heard, though she was having some immature feelings right now. She had no right to expect anything from Adam. He had no right to expect anything from her.

Except casual politeness.

He'd manipulated Erica into the sling and had hoisted the diaper bag. She couldn't help but smile when she looked at it.

"Don't say it," he joked. "It's not quite my style."

She remembered how he'd been flirting with Carla. "That look seems to be working for you."

He cocked his head at her words and studied her. "I read your article in the paper last night. You did a nice job."

"Thank you. I hope it does some good." Then, feeling uncomfortable, she asked, "Did you find the workshop worthwhile?"

"The question-and-answer session was. And I took good notes to give to Tina for when Erica's about six months old. I'll get them off my phone when I get back and leave her a list along with the handouts Mary furnished."

He was still planning on leaving. He still thought Tina would return and everything would work out fine. She wished she could believe that, too.

Kaitlyn stiffened as Carla approached them, all sunshine, blond hair, blue eyes and pretty baby.

Somehow, despite holding her diaper bag and her daughter, she touched Adam's arm again. "We'll have to have a playdate for the kids. We can compare notes."

Kaitlyn expected some kind of flirtatious response, but Adam politely said, "I'm not going to be in town long. As I mentioned in the group, I'm just taking care of Erica for my sister."

Carla looked disappointed, but then she returned with, "Will we see you here next week?"

Adam nodded. "Yes, you will. Unless my sister is back."

After a warm goodbye, Carla left the room.

Kaitlyn suddenly realized why Adam might not be interested. Carla had a baby. Wasn't that what he was trying to leave behind?

Not knowing exactly what had gotten into her, Kaitlyn asked, "Not a dating prospect?"

He arched a brow. "As you reminded me more than once, not when I'm leaving for Thailand in a month."

"And a baby isn't in your plans," she murmured.

Looking a little annoyed, he responded, "Not when one is already disrupting my life."

She'd asked for it, and she'd gotten it. Adam and babies weren't a permanent combination. It really was time to make her exit.

Acting as a doctor would with any patient, she smiled, said, "I'm glad the workshop was helpful," and left him standing there with a group of new moms.

Kaitlyn's breath caught as she saw Adam come into the winery's community hall Friday evening. He was imposingly masculine in a tuxedo. He was also unbelievably sexy. However, she hadn't been able to forget what he'd said about Erica being a disruption in his life. Kaitlyn could never look at a child that way... not ever.

Before she and Adam made eye contact, Jase approached her. "I have some exciting news."

"What news would that be?"

"Your article in the paper and on our website was popular and caught lots of attention."

"I don't understand."

"Have you checked the comments section?"

"No, I haven't had time."

"Spoken like a busy physician." He shook his head. "A TV station in L.A. wants to do an interview with you. They think you'd make the perfect human interest piece."

"I don't *want* to be a human interest piece."

"I know you don't. But think about what this interview can do for other women if they identify with your story. Think about what this interview could do for The Mommy Club. Think of other towns that might set up similar organizations."

"How long do I have to think about it?"

"Twenty-four hours. You strike when the iron is hot with publicity."

"Would I have to go to L.A.?"

"No. They'd come here. I think they want the small-town feel. Local shots of the town...you in your hometown setting. That kind of thing."

"Do you know the interviewer?"

"Boy, you know the right questions to ask. I know her by reputation. She's honest and direct. Actually,

I think Tanya Edwards is a divorced single mom herself. My guess is that's why she wanted to do this."

Adam was approaching them now, and Kaitlyn felt her heart begin to race. This wasn't a matter of willpower. Her body just responded to him.

After Jase and Adam exchanged greetings, Jase said to Kaitlyn, "We'll talk about it again later," and went to the table where Kaitlyn would be sitting, too. The room was beautifully equipped with round tables and white linens, a buffet layout and a wine-tasting bar. Instead of a runway for the bachelors, Marissa had simply set up a dais with two mikes. A bachelor could introduce himself and then Marissa would auction him off. Kaitlyn wondered who would bid on Adam and what kind of price he'd bring. Mentally, she kicked herself. She really shouldn't care.

"Can you give me a couple of minutes?" Adam asked as he nodded toward a quiet corner.

The compelling intent in his eyes urged her to take a breath and then nod. He steered her to a table where a flower arrangement towered. Brochures about The Mommy Club fanned around it.

"I gave you the wrong impression on Wednesday."

When she just waited, he blew out a breath. "I wouldn't be honest if I didn't admit Erica has been a surprising disruption in my life. But she hasn't been an altogether unwelcome one."

At that, Kaitlyn knew her surprise must have shown.

"I never realized how much responsibility, let alone logistics, goes into being a single parent. Just carrying a diaper bag and a baby can be a challenge. And all the questions the new mothers had at the workshop made me worry about Tina even more. I know what you said about trusting Tina to come back on her own, but I know a private investigator in one of the companies my firm contracts with. He's discreet and he's good. I have to do something, Kaitlyn."

"You have to do something because you want to leave in a few weeks?"

"I have a contractual responsibility in a few weeks. Certainly you can understand that."

Yes, she could. If she suddenly couldn't see patients, the other doctors in the practice would have to take over for her. Adam didn't have anyone to take over for him.

"But my main reason for wanting to find her is simply to find her, to reunite her with Erica, to figure out what she needs to be a mom. Jade was a good mother to her. She didn't neglect her even after she married Dad. Maybe that's one of the reasons her marriage didn't work out. Tina still came first. So Tina knows how to be a good mom. She just needs a chance to do it."

Kaitlyn felt her heart melting. Everything he was saying made sense, and the truth was, she didn't have the experience of being a single parent, so she could only imagine his frustration.

"Are you saying you might even enjoy taking care of Erica…a little?"

He chuckled. "I'm saying we're actually communicating. She looks at me with those big blue eyes and I talk to her. But afterward I wonder why am I talking to a two-month-old baby."

"Because she's growing into a little person. Did you leave her with someone on my list?"

"Mary Garcia's watching her. After you left the workshop, I spoke to her for a while. I told her about tonight and that I didn't like the idea of a stranger watching Erica. So she offered. She has a nursing degree, so Erica's in good hands."

Kaitlyn had known that about Mary, but was surprised Adam had taken the time to find out. He was acting more and more like a dad every day, even if he might be reluctant to be one.

"You and Jase seemed pretty intense. I hope I didn't interrupt anything," he said.

"You didn't."

Adam waited as if he expected her to confide in him. Is that what intimacy did? Made expectations more real? And if he expected that of her, what did she expect of him? Nothing. Absolutely nothing. That way she couldn't get her heart broken.

"Jase wants me to do a TV interview with someone from L.A. It would focus on my background and how I got involved in The Mommy Club."

"I meant it when I said your article was good. And as for TV…" He paused and gave her a wicked grin. "You're very photogenic."

She felt herself blushing and didn't know what to say to that.

He laughed. "Sometimes I think you forget you're a beautiful woman as well as a pediatrician." He hooked his arm in hers. "Come on. Let's take our seats. I think they're about to start the program."

Marissa was headed for the dais. As the hostess, as well as auctioneer for the evening, she looked the part in a beaded green cocktail dress with her curly black hair piled high on her head. After being Jase's assistant at the winery, she'd fallen into this job of planning the events. She was so good at it Jase had said he was afraid someone else would steal her away.

But Kaitlyn's attention soon went from Marissa to the feel of Adam's hand on her waist as he guided her toward their table. She wished she could be immune to his touch, but she simply wasn't. All she could do was not let it show. No matter which way she turned the situation, she knew Adam would be leaving, not just this once but again and again. If she could settle for an affair—

Even in the worst days of her marriage, an affair wasn't something she'd ever wanted.

After Marissa gave an introduction, she thanked Jase and Sara for hosting the event and explained a little bit about The Mommy Club. Then she invited everyone to enjoy the food. In addition to the buffet setup, waiters brought around hors d'oeuvres and glasses of wine or sparkling cider. During the preauction social time, Kaitlyn was terrifically aware of Adam beside her, of his elbow brushing hers, of his deep voice as he conversed with Sara, Jase and the other people around them. Marissa fluttered here and there like a sparkling bird once food was being served, and Kaitlyn thought about Marissa's history, the father of her baby and how far her friend had come.

An hour later, the auction began. One of the doctors in Kaitlyn's practice was up first. When he went up to the dais, she gave him a thumbs-up sign. He grinned back and eventually went for a bid of two thousand dollars.

She had to decide whether or not she was going to bid on Adam. One little voice in her head told her she should, another little voice in her head told her she shouldn't. She was going to babysit for him if he went out on a date with someone else. Wouldn't *that* be awkward?

Still, that wasn't a good reason to bid on him. She didn't want him to think she wanted to continue what had happened between them.

It was a dilemma, and one she had to solve quickly because Marissa, at the mike, said, "Our next bachelor up for auction is Adam Preston. Adam, come on up and tell us about yourself."

Once on the dais, he said into the mike, "I'm Adam Preston, an environmental geologist, and an eligible bachelor."

Kaitlyn crossed her arms over her breasts. She was *not* going to bid.

Chapter Seven

Adam stood in front of the crowd feeling altogether foolish. Yes, he was used to wearing a tuxedo. Yes, he was used to giving lectures in front of an auditorium full of college students. Yes, he walked teams through procedures when they approached a job site. But he'd never stood in front of a group like this, mostly women, waiting for one of them to bid on him.

Barbaric. That's what it was.

However, when his gaze fell on Kaitlyn, he knew it was for a worthy cause, so he smiled broadly and turned toward Marissa.

"And what is an environmental geologist, Adam?" Marissa asked so the crowd could get to know him a little more.

"I try to bring water to drought-ravaged areas of the world. But in my everyday life, I'm just an ordinary guy from Fawn Grove who'd be glad to take someone out to dinner and a movie and have a fun evening for a good cause."

"How old are you?" a woman shouted out.

He laughed. "I'm thirty-two and counting."

With a smile, Marissa added, "He's six-two, has green eyes, and I think those shoulders probably fill out a forty-six jacket."

Everybody laughed this time.

Marissa winked at him and Adam knew this was all in good fun. Suddenly he felt more comfortable.

His gaze met Kaitlyn's. Would she bid on him?

He doubted it. That would be making some kind of public statement. He couldn't forget making love with her no matter how hard he tried. She seemed to be in his thoughts day and night, when he wasn't worrying about Tina. Even when he took care of Erica, he remembered how Kaitlyn had held her, how she'd cooed to her, had rocked her. How she'd clung to *him*...

For the past week, he'd felt as if he'd been under some kind of spell, either a baby spell or a Kaitlyn Foster spell. He wasn't sure which was worse.

Marissa called for bids. Standing in the spotlight, he couldn't see everyone who was bidding. Entering into the fun of the auction, Marissa said, "Maybe Adam could unbutton his jacket."

The audience clapped and he shook his head. *All in good fun,* he reminded himself, unbuttoning his tux, slipping off the jacket, and hooking it over his shoulder.

There was applause again and a few more bids.

"We're at two thousand dollars, and I'm sure someone wants to go a little higher. Come on, ladies."

There was a shout from a back corner, "Twenty-five hundred."

Adam thought the voice sounded a little familiar, but seeing into the crowd was difficult.

When Marissa announced, "Going once, going twice, sold to paddle number fifty-two," Adam didn't know who had bought the evening with him. He just knew it wasn't Kaitlyn. There was a sharp stab of disappointment, but he smiled and waved and slipped on his jacket once more. Then he went down the stairs to the table where the settling up was done to meet the winning bidder.

To his surprise, he realized he *had* recognized that voice—a voice from his past—Sherry Conniff. Eleven years had changed her, but he still recognized the beautiful girl she'd been, the one who'd stolen his heart and trampled on it so completely way back when. Her black-as-night hair was braided about her head in a coronet. Her model-perfect posture straightened her shoulders. She was dressed to kill in a siren-red dress, but her hazel eyes were serious as she studied him warily.

He couldn't say he was glad to see her. There was bitterness and resentment there that he'd tried to erase but hadn't been able to.

Without preliminaries he asked, "Why did you bid on me?"

She hesitated a moment. "Because I thought our conversation was long overdue. I've wanted to apologize all these years, Adam, but the truth is, I didn't know how. I saw your bio and photo in the Sacramento paper and that's why I came to bid on you. I know this is no place to talk. I thought we could save that for to-morrow night, if you'll go out with me."

He had once loved her as a young man could love, and those feelings tugged at him. "How are you doing?"

"I suppose you heard I got my law degree?"

"The grapevine mentioned it. You've been practicing in Sacramento, haven't you?"

"I have. I'm with a great firm specializing in international law. I'm on the partner track, which is just what I've always wanted. Most weeks, I work sixty hours or more. But this is what I've wanted since I was twelve, Adam, and you knew that."

"I knew you wanted to please your father."

She took his hand and just held it gently. "Let's not get into any of that now. Can we wait until tomorrow night?"

"So you don't expect me to escort you to your seat and spend tonight with you, too?"

"Of course not. You came with people tonight, didn't you?"

At first he found he wanted to say no, that he'd come alone. But then he remembered Jase and Sara and the way she'd convinced him to do this. He remembered Kaitlyn offering to babysit, and Marissa trying every way she could to make the night easy on him.

"Where are you living?" he asked. "I'll have to know where to pick you up. Around 7:00 p.m.?"

Sherry gave him her card, a Sacramento address. He wasn't looking forward to an evening with her. Not at all. But maybe it was time for this. Maybe it was time he closed the door on resentment and bitterness and made peace with his past.

* * *

As he returned to the table, Kaitlyn turned a questioning gaze on him. How awkward was this?

Awkward or not, he thought he owed Kaitlyn some explanation.

However, Sara was the one who broke the sudden, stifling silence between them. "You set the bar high for all the guys coming after you. Liam's going to be nervous now."

Adam shrugged. "It could be that the donation bids will go up after each bachelor."

Although he wanted to leave, although what he really wanted to do was to take Kaitlyn back to his condo and make love to her all over again, he sat down beside her.

"That was an experience," he said to Kaitlyn as she sipped her water, appearing unconcerned about what had happened.

"You looked comfortable up there."

"Well, I wasn't. We all pretend when we have to."

Now she gave him a curious regard. "You don't have to pretend to be handsome and debonair and charming. You just are."

That statement completely took him aback. "You make it sound like a *bad* thing. Or are you upset because *you* seem to think those qualities are attractive?" How could she deny that when she'd responded to him the way she had?

"Any woman in here would give her eyeteeth to be seen on your arm in a nice restaurant."

"Including you?"

"I'm not impressed by expensive restaurants."

"Is that why you didn't bid?"

"I didn't bid because…" She shrugged and shook her head, looking more vulnerable than he'd ever seen her.

He leaned close and practically murmured in her ear, "Kaitlyn, what happened between us was special. Maybe you don't want to admit that, but I can. You don't have to bid on me to go out with me. I'd take you anywhere, anytime."

And if she thought those words had a double meaning, she was probably right.

She blushed and leaned away slightly. "How can you be thinking about taking me out when you just made a date with someone else?"

"You're the woman I'd like to go out with, but I have an obligation now and I'll keep it."

"Do you know her?"

There it was. She'd been watching and she'd seen the tension or connection or whatever it was between him and Sherry.

"Yes, I know her," he admitted. "Her name is Sherry Conniff."

Recognition dawned in Kaitlyn's eyes. "She's the girl who was in the accident with you."

He glanced around to make sure no one was listening.

"Yes," he said simply.

Kaitlyn didn't ask any more questions. He didn't supply any more information. More coffee came and went. Jase and Sara picked up the conversation. Soon he couldn't abide sitting there any longer. He stood.

"So when's your date?" Sara asked before he could leave.

"It's tomorrow night."

As if she were assuring him she kept her obliga-
tions, too, Kaitlyn said, "I can keep Erica at your place.
What time do you need me there?"

He wanted to say, *I'll get any other babysitter but
you. You don't understand this at all though you think
you do. Kaitlyn, stop being so afraid and make love
with me again.* But he didn't say any of those things.
He said, "If you can be there at six-thirty, that will
be great."

After Kaitlyn nodded, he said his goodbyes, then
left, feeling as if he had tumbled down a rabbit hole
and couldn't find his way out.

Kaitlyn brought plenty of work along to keep her
occupied while Adam was on his date. Good thing,
too, because Erica had gone to sleep after her dinner
feeding and Kaitlyn didn't want to think about what
had happened between her and Adam here.

Now, however, she pushed those thoughts—along
with her laptop—aside and rubbed her eyes and closed
her computer.

Adam had said all the right things before he'd left
on his date—call him if she needed him, call him if
Erica wouldn't settle down. She had his cell phone
number, of course, but he'd also given her the name
and number of the restaurant where he expected to be.
It was upper-level expensive, just the kind of place a
bachelor auction date would require.

So why did she get the feeling this was more than a
date? Why was she almost queasy with the thought of
him gazing into Sherry Conniff's eyes across a table
for two? Just what did she *want* from Adam?

That was the question she most certainly didn't

know the answer to. She just knew she shouldn't be so attracted. She shouldn't want to melt into his arms. She shouldn't want him to make love to her all over again.

When she heard the key in the lock shortly after ten o'clock, she was surprised. That was a short evening. Maybe he was bringing Sherry Conniff back here. Wouldn't *that* be awkward?

She tried to prepare herself for any eventuality as the door opened and Adam came in. At first she could read nothing from his expression.

After a quick glance around, seeing the portable crib wasn't anywhere in sight, he remarked, "I guess Erica's sleeping in the bedroom."

"I stayed in there awhile with her after she first fell asleep. I didn't want to pull her in here and change her usual routine."

"When she falls asleep, she usually doesn't care where she is. It's getting her to sleep that's the trick. What time did she go down?"

"About an hour ago. She had a fussy spell but we played and walked through it."

"I'm going to check on her," he said. "I'll be right back."

Kaitlyn slipped her laptop into its leather case and zippered it.

By then Adam was back. He'd discarded his suit jacket and tugged down his tie. A few curling hairs peeked out from his open shirt collar. He was as sexy tonight as he'd been at the bachelor auction. He was sexy *any* night. In spite of her desire to lock the memories away, she could remember touching him so well. She could remember tasting him even better.

Taking a deep breath and squaring her shoulders,

remembering he'd been out with another woman, she asked, "How was your date?"

His answer was slow in coming, but told her nothing at all. "We had a great dinner."

"So this date was just about a great dinner?"

"You're going on a fishing expedition, Kaitlyn, and you're using an awfully long line. Do you want to shorten it a bit?"

She couldn't tell if he was annoyed, angry or impatient. "I was just wondering how long it had been since you'd seen Sherry."

Her heart beat three times until he said, "It's been eleven years."

Now *that* she hadn't expected. "So her bid at the bachelor auction was a complete surprise?"

"Yes, it was. Almost as much a surprise as your not bidding at all."

Whoa. What did she hear in his voice? Disappointment? "Adam, I didn't know how to react after what happened. I was confused and upset."

He pounced on that last word. "Upset?"

"I'm a doctor, for goodness' sake. I know I need to use protection."

"Unless you were so involved in passion and desire, protection was the last thought on your mind for the first time in your life."

Was that what had happened to *him,* too?

They seemed to be breathing in unison. They seemed to be gravitating toward each other when Adam's cell phone beeped. As he shot it a dark look, Kaitlyn suspected he was thinking about letting the call go to voice mail. But when he lifted it from his belt to check the screen, she saw hope flare in his eyes.

"It's Tina," he muttered. He answered the call with "Tina?"

Kaitlyn thought he might go to the bedroom for privacy, but he stayed right there. "Don't hang up," he ordered her.

This was big brother Adam taking charge and Kaitlyn wondered if that would work. She hoped it would.

He listened for what seemed like a long while, even though it was probably only a couple of minutes. Kaitlyn found she was almost as worried about his sister as he was.

Kaitlyn's heart cracked a bit when he said, "Please don't cry. Tina, everything's going to be all right." There was a pause and then in a firm voice he said, "I won't give up on you, and I won't let anything happen to Erica, either."

His sister must have been either crying or telling him something he didn't want to hear, because he was shaking his head. Suddenly he took the phone from his ear and stared at it. Then he swore. "She hung up."

"But she called and talked to you this time. That means something, doesn't it?"

As he studied Kaitlyn, some of the tension went out of his shoulders. "Yes, it does. It means my progress reports are making a difference. It means she's thinking about Erica every day. It means maybe she'll come home."

Kaitlyn studied him then, fully aware of how much he was hurting, of how much he was worried. "So what exactly did she say?"

"She said she needs more time. She's not sure she can be a single mom. I tried to reassure her. I can tell she just feels...alone. That's my fault."

If she told him it wasn't, he wouldn't believe her. She took a step even closer, but then she abruptly stopped. She smelled perfume on his shirt as if—

"Kaitlyn, what's wrong?"

She stepped away from him. "Nothing."

"Don't tell me nothing when something obviously is."

"I can smell a woman's perfume on you."

He sighed. "You smell Sherry's perfume, and because you do, you're drawing conclusions. I assure you, they're the wrong ones."

"Maybe you should enlighten me."

"Oh, I'd like to, Kaitlyn, I really would. Even more than enlighten you, I'd like to make love to you again. But now you have some cockeyed idea that I reignited old sparks with Sherry and you're using that as another excuse to back off."

"You don't know what I'm thinking," she shot back.

"Am I close?" he asked with a faint undertone of anger, as if he'd had a very frustrating night and this was just the close of it.

"Yes, you're close. I'm not going to try to hug you or get close to you when you've been with another woman an hour before."

"*Been* with another woman," he repeated gruffly. "I was with Sherry, who has felt guilty for eleven years for pursuing her own dreams at my expense. She had decided that I hate her. When I told her I forgive her, she got all teary-eyed and gave me a long hug. That's the short story and the long one."

With a studied look and precise determination, Kaitlyn returned, "I don't think it's long enough. Tell me what happened that night. Tell me why you were blamed, but she feels guilty. Don't act as if it isn't that important," she warned.

"Oh, I know how important it is." Then he fell silent, and his expression warned her not to ask more questions.

Kaitlyn was never impulsive. She was never a risk taker. Yet tonight, she was both of those things.

Maybe it was too many pent-up emotions that led her to say, "I might think what happened between us was a mistake. But that doesn't keep me from wanting to know you. Tell me what happened that night. Tell me why she bid twenty-five hundred dollars on you. Tell me why she feels guilty, rather than *you* feeling guilty."

"Why does it matter?"

"It matters because I want to know the man behind the story, the man behind Tina, the man behind the childhood that sucked."

"All right," he said warily. "All right." He sank down on the sofa and she sat beside him.

"It's a simple story," he said, studying the carpet. "I'm sure I'm not the first one in this position, nor will be the last."

"I want to hear it," she said gently, wanting to touch him yet knowing this wasn't the time.

"We went to a party on holiday break. Sherry had picked me up, because she'd gotten a new car. She was from Sacramento, a stone's throw away. I loved that girl as much as a guy could love a girl at that age. Jade and Dad divorced. Tina was lost, calling me for advice and reassurance. Sherry gave me an escape. Only I wanted to escape *to* Sherry. What twenty-one-year-old with roiling hormones wouldn't? She was smart, beautiful and sexy."

He stared off into space as if remembering that time of his life with perfect recall. "She intended to become a lawyer. Although I almost had a B.S. under my belt, I had no idea what *I* intended to become. I had no burning goal. She did. She was determined to fly through law school, become a partner and build a reputation. She'd talked about it since I'd met her. I admired her. I would have done anything for her."

"What *did* you do for her?" Kaitlyn asked, prompting him to confide in her.

"I lied for her," he said, simply. "We went to that party. I had a couple of beers, but she was doing shots. I told her to slow down, but she didn't. She got behind the wheel before I could stop her and I hopped in with her hoping...hoping that I could control something. My sin that night was letting her drive. I kept my seat belt off so I could grab the wheel if I needed to, I guess. I don't even know anymore. The accident happened so fast, in less than a blink of an eye. She took a curve too fast and the car overturned. It was a convertible and we were both thrown from it. I was lucky not to get hurt. She wasn't."

Kaitlyn moved closer to him then. Did she think combining their body heat would give him some comfort all these years later? She wanted more than closeness, and that wanting urged her to clasp his arm. "What happened to Sherry?"

"She had a concussion and had to have immediate surgery. The surgeon removed her spleen. She had a broken leg, too, and it was all my fault because I didn't take her keys."

"It was *her* fault because she drove."

"I can see that now. I couldn't then. So when the police and paramedics showed up, I said I'd been driving."

"Oh, Adam."

"I liked her, Kaitlyn. I would have done anything for her. She wanted to go to law school. *Law* school. She couldn't have a DUI on her record. So I said I was driving and there you have it."

"But that's not the end of the story, is it?"

He looked directly at her now. "I don't know what you mean."

"Yes, you do. You loved her. You hoped she'd come forward and tell the truth. But she never did, did she?"

"I don't think she even thought about it. After the accident, her parents wouldn't let her see me. I tried calling her, but she wouldn't take my calls. She didn't set the record straight. I told myself that was okay. She had goals…I didn't. But deep down, it wasn't okay, and I felt more betrayed than I'd ever felt before. If what Jade and my dad shared or what Sherry and I had shared was love, I wanted no part of *that,* either."

"And in all these years she never got in touch with you?"

"Nope. Not until she bid on me last night. She told me she felt we needed to settle things. So we made the date for tonight."

"So did you?"

He shook his head. "It was too late to settle anything. Sherry kept apologizing. She said after the accident and me being charged with reckless driving, she felt too ashamed and guilty to get in touch with me. Her family acted as if it were my father's duty to pay for her medical bills, and he did. But what they didn't know was that I worked my tail off to pay a good share of them. What had happened was *my* responsibility, not his."

"And for all these years, you couldn't set the record straight because it would affect her."

"Exactly."

"Adam, I'm sorry that happened to you. I'm sorry you felt so betrayed."

He obviously could hear the sincerity in her voice and that must have prodded him to say again, "You smell her perfume on me because of a hug."

Had her jealousy been so obvious? "I'm sorry I jumped to conclusions."

"Maybe I've been purposely giving you the wrong impression all along," Adam admitted.

Her throat went dry because the conversation seemed to be a vital one. She managed to ask, "Why?"

"Because getting involved isn't practical."

"And we should be practical," she agreed halfheartedly, seeing the desire in his eyes, feeling it in her whole body.

"Yes, we should," he said, but his actions didn't match his words. He leaned down and kissed her.

Adam's kisses could seduce her in a second. This one was slow and coaxing until anticipation filled her world. Without half trying, his kiss convinced her there was no place else she'd rather be, and no one else she'd rather be with.

In the space of a breath, they needed their bodies as close as they could be. What he'd confided to her was deeply personal and deeply wrenching. It told her better than anything else could why he was restless, why he didn't stay in one place, why roots and love and a family seemed foreign to him. He didn't want them because love and bonds and connections brought pain. She'd felt the pain from love and bonds, too. The difference was that she still wanted them.

Adam broke away. But he didn't let go. Rather he leaned his forehead against hers.

"Any more of that and we'll soon be naked. Is that what you want?"

Shakily she managed to say, "That wouldn't be very practical, would it?"

"No, it wouldn't be practical at all. I can give you desire. I can give you pleasure. I can give us a few short weeks."

Desire, pleasure and a few short weeks. Would she risk her heart for those? Would she risk her heart for the opportunity to make love with Adam again? That wasn't a decision she was prepared to make tonight. That wasn't a decision she was prepared to make in the afterglow of one of his kisses.

"I like you, Adam," she said breathlessly, as if she were declaring her first crush.

He smiled. "I like you, too. Maybe liking each other has to be enough for now."

He didn't look too happy about that, but she could see his better sense agreed.

"Will you be at Thrifty Solutions tomorrow?" he asked her. "I know a group of volunteers are gathering to unpack boxes and label things. I told Sara I'd help unload the truck. She assured me she'd watch Erica while I do."

"Yes, I'm planning on helping. I'm glad you volunteered. Sara was afraid it would be too much for Jase to handle on his own."

"She'd better not let Jase hear that."

Kaitlyn laughed. "Male egos have to be protected at all cost."

She remembered Tom and the things he'd said to her at the end, and realized maybe she hadn't protected his. Maybe that's the real reason why their marriage had broken apart.

"What's wrong?" Adam asked.

"Nothing's wrong," she said, almost believing it. "I'm going to go."

He didn't say she shouldn't. He didn't pull her into his arms again to keep her there.

So she picked up her laptop case and headed to the door. And this time when she left, she wondered if she wasn't making the biggest mistake of her life.

Chapter Eight

While unpacking clothes on Sunday afternoon, deciding what rack they would go on, labeling and pricing them, Kaitlyn spotted Adam walk through the door from her vantage point in Thrifty Solutions' storeroom. He was carrying his niece in her sling.

As if by magnetic pull, Adam's gaze sought hers across the salesroom. Crossing to the storeroom, he smiled. She got caught up in that smile.

"Have you been here long?" he asked, patting Erica's back, but keeping his focus on Kaitlyn.

"About an hour." She shouldn't feel breathless. She shouldn't feel as if she wanted to lean forward to kiss him. The intense desire in his eyes told her he might be thinking about kissing her, too.

"Our getting-ready-to-leave routine took longer than I expected." He dropped Erica's diaper bag and clasped Kaitlyn's arm as if he wanted some physical contact. The touch of his fingers on her skin reminded her of everything they'd done together. He leaned close to her and, in a low voice, said, "I want to ask you something. But right now, I'm going to turn Erica over to Sara and help unload that truck."

After a squeeze of her arm, he picked up Erica's bag and went to Sara, handing over Erica and the bag.

Kaitlyn felt as if *she* wanted to be the one watching Erica. But that was silly. Erica wasn't hers. Adam wasn't hers. Still, she felt proprietary of both of them. Just what did he want to ask her?

In the baby section of Thrifty Solutions, there was a swing much like the one Adam used at his condo. Sara settled Erica in that.

Adam spoke to Erica for a couple of minutes. Not just nonsense, either, but gentle words about being right there and that he'd be back soon and Sara was going to play with her. All things a dad would say. Did he even realize that?

Kaitlyn was sorting blouses according to their sizes and dressiness when Adam went to the garage-type door where a truck had backed in to unload. When he returned inside, he had three boxes stacked on top of each other on a dolly.

He unloaded them onto the floor and looked around the racks that Kaitlyn had been setting up. "Where does all this come from?" he asked.

"That's hard to say. The Mommy Club started with one original benefactress. No one knows who she is. She set up the foundation to draw on for anything families might need. Then that foundation endowed this thrift store and bought storage units where volunteers can stow furniture that families might be able to use. There are many benefactors now. Anyone who's helped by The Mommy Club usually gives back. It's a circle that never stops."

"Sort of like a wedding ring," Adam mused.

Kaitlyn jerked her head up, surprised to hear that come from him. With his kiss too much on her mind, with making love with him always on her mind, she wondered how much he thought about marriage. She knew he didn't think much of it.

"What makes you say that?" she asked.

"Wedding rings are supposed to symbolize the never-ending circle that keeps two people united for a lifetime. As long as each does their part, the circle stays intact. But if somebody doesn't, that circle breaks open.

"I've seen good marriages work," she said, that old dream still tugging at her.

"Have you? So far I've only seen Jase and Sara's and they haven't been married very long."

She considered Jase and Sara. "That golden circle is protection when the rough times come. That's when you have to hold on tighter and make sure it doesn't break. Mine did and I still wish there was something I would have been able to do about that."

"Do you still wish you were married?"

"I wish my marriage had survived. I wish it could have been all we'd dreamed it should be."

Adam left the stack of boxes and came close to where she was standing at the rack. He was wearing jeans and a T-shirt today. His hair was tousled, and there was some beard stubble on his chin as if he'd rushed this morning, but he looked altogether sexy, and her heart was jumping around like a wild teen-ager's at a rock concert.

Get a grip, girl, she told herself. But how could she when she remembered his body on hers, his body inside of hers.

"I'd like to ask you something personal," he said.

"You can ask."

"I know what *that* means. If you don't want to an-swer, you won't. That's fine." He paused a beat, then he asked, "Do you still love your ex?"

That question caught her totally off guard. Was *this* what he wanted to ask her? "Love Tom?"

Adam just waited, studying her face, gazing into her eyes. He'd confided in her and now he expected the same of her.

"Tom was smart and wanted to know everything about the world. We had deep discussions, maybe more than we laughed together. I missed my mom and dad. Maybe that's why I married him. I thought our lives would fit together like puzzle pieces, but they didn't. Before I got pregnant, I think we both knew we were growing apart. He was having trouble accepting my professional life. I was having trouble accepting the social events he wanted to go to. Our lives were shifting under our feet. He was my first serious relationship, and because of that, I'll always think of him fondly. But love…the love we once felt for each other is gone."

"You're sure about that? Maybe you still love him, and that's the reason you can't move on."

"Who says I can't move on?" she protested.

"*You* say it every time you run."

There was no escaping the certainty in his voice. "And what would you do if I stopped running?"

"It would be fascinating to find out, wouldn't it?"

Jase had hopped off the truck and wheeled in another dolly load of boxes. "The interview is on Tuesday at four. You got my email?"

"I got it," she said. She'd checked her emails quickly this morning and hadn't had time to answer them. "I just don't know how much I really want to go into on TV. That seems so much different than writing."

"Are you nervous?" Adam asked.

"I guess I am. I shouldn't be. Jase tells me the interviewer will be sympathetic."

"Would you like me to be there for moral support?"

The longer she was with Adam, the more she wanted to *be* with him. He could have a calming effect on her. He could help her keep her perspective. "Yes," she responded to his question, feeling as if she was committing herself to…something.

Sara had walked Erica over to where Kaitlyn, Adam and her husband were standing. She said to the baby, "See. I told you Uncle Adam was right here. He's not going to leave you."

"I can probably bring her along to the interview," Adam said. "But I *am* going to need a sitter for tomorrow night. I give a lecture at Wilson University."

"I'd be glad to babysit her," Sara offered. "Marissa and Jordan are coming over for dinner."

"Are you sure that's okay? Three kids to watch?"

"We're fine. Babies stay where you put them."

When Sara moved away with Erica again and Jase went outside, Adam turned back to Kaitlyn.

"Are you busy tomorrow night?"

"I don't have any plans."

"Would you like to come with me? You might be bored, but you'd learn a little more about what an environmental geologist does, and the careers the students are planning to move into. What do you think?"

"I think I'd like to go along to see a different side of you." Adam was a fascinating man and, in spite of herself, she was intrigued by him.

"No different sides. I like what I do, and you'll see that."

Somehow they were standing close together again. Adam looked like he wanted to kiss her, and she certainly wanted to kiss him. But Jase or Sara could be back at any minute. He seemed to realize that, too. He cleared his throat and said, "We'll have time together tomorrow night."

She was looking forward to that. Maybe a little too much.

On Monday evening, Adam watched Kaitlyn as Marissa's little boy, Jordan, ran toward her with a giggle and wrapped his little arms around one leg.

She laughed, scooped him up and asked, "So what are you having for supper?"

There was a streak of cheesy sauce across his lip and on his hand.

"Careful," Marissa told her, hurrying over with a wet paper towel. "I was just going to wash him up. He got his fingers into the macaroni and cheese."

"A little yellow with this pattern isn't going to make a difference," Kaitlyn returned with a smile.

Adam was always amazed at Kaitlyn's aplomb with kids, and he wasn't sure why. Maybe because he hadn't witnessed many women who were good with children. Most of the women he'd dated seemed adverse to babies. But Kaitlyn didn't hesitate to wrap her arms around them. Neither did Marissa or Sara.

Standing by the sink, Sara came forward now to take Erica from his arms. He was finding it harder and harder to allow Erica to be in someone else's care. He wanted to make sure nothing ever happened to her.

He handed over Erica saying, "I'll bring in her portable crib."

Five minutes later he'd set it up in the cavernous kitchen. Jase and Sara had moved into this house with Jase's dad, Ethan, after some renovations were completed. It was certainly big enough for everyone to wander around. From the table, Sara's daughter, Amy, grinned at him as she spooned macaroni and cheese into her mouth. Adam bet the flower arrangement on the table came from the nearby gardens. He thought about his condo, how sterile it seemed compared to this. If he ever had kids—

Kids? Really? What was he thinking?

Still, a family needed grounding. A family needed a house. Maybe not one as grand as this, but one that was welcoming and gave everyone a sense of belonging.

He'd never felt as if he belonged anywhere. Maybe divorce just did that to kids.

Marissa had seated Jordan in his high chair and was spooning a little more macaroni and cheese onto his dish.

"You'd think we'd be eating something more nutritious," Sara said with a laugh. "But Amy and Jordan like mac and cheese as much as French fries and we gave in for tonight."

Adam plopped the diaper bag on the counter. "Everything you need should be in here."

"What I need," Marissa said, "is a book on plumbing. How do you fix a leaky sink? I was going to ask Jase how to do it, but he's stuck in a meeting with Liam."

"A leaky sink? I can take care of that," Adam assured her. "I was looking for a way to pay you back for watching Erica tonight. How about I stop by tomorrow morning?"

"Oh, you don't have to—" Marissa began.

But Kaitlyn stopped her. "Adam doesn't like to owe anyone. I'm sure he could fix it for you."

"That would be great then. I'm sure Jase will let me take a few hours." After a pause, Marissa looked from one of them to the other and smiled. "Are you two dating?" she asked bluntly.

They answered in unison, "No."

Sara and Marissa exchanged a look.

Sara said under her breath, "Well, something's in the air. But if you say you're not dating, I'll believe you." She looked at Kaitlyn. "So you're just going along to listen to his lecture?"

Kaitlyn blushed a little. "Yep." That's all she said.

Two and a half hours later, Adam thought about Sara's comments as he guided Kaitlyn into a campus coffee shop after his lecture. Dating was such an old-fashioned term, yet he found himself wanting to spend more time with Kaitlyn. Wasn't that what tonight was all about? Wasn't that what a date was all about?

As they gave their orders and took their coffees to a table for two, Adam realized he and Kaitlyn had started their relationship backward. Of course, the night he'd kissed her at the winery, he'd never realized they might have a relationship.

Adam was black coffee all the way, and he discovered Kaitlyn was, too.

They sat elbow to elbow. She said, "Your subject matter really is fascinating."

"You mean you didn't catch any of the students sleeping?"

She laughed. "No. They were all interested and engaged, and the question-and-answer session got really lively. They liked you."

"You sound as if that's unusual."

"I don't know. Some of the lectures that I sat through in med school were so impersonal. But yours wasn't. You kept them involved. That's the sign of a good teacher."

"I enjoy it when I make the time to do it. And the head of the department tries to hire me every time he sees me. Actually, on the job site, I'm teaching more than I think I am. When I start out on a new project, sometimes I don't even know my team, so I have to feel my way with instructions and questions and let them have input. It's sort of like a college lecture."

She studied him for a long moment until he finally asked, "What?"

"You're not at all what I expected," she said.

"Expected?" He couldn't keep the amusement from his voice.

"At the winery the night I met you, you were dressed in an expensive suit, you knew just what to say, you were a great conversationalist. You acted like a…jet-setter."

"Is that why I swept you away?"

She shook her head. "I wasn't swept away."

At his arched brow, she admitted, "Maybe a little swept away. I just hadn't expected a man to make me feel so…special. Not after everything that had happened."

"You told me a little about your marriage, about what you'd written in the article. Now tell me what wasn't there. Tell me what really split you up."

He hadn't expected the conversation to turn this serious. After all, if it was a date, and it seemed close to it, he'd wanted Kaitlyn to have a good time. But for some reason, he had to know more about her marriage.

"You told me your story, and now I have to tell you mine?" she asked, looking more unsure than he'd ever seen her.

"You don't have to, Kaitlyn, but would it hurt to share a little bit about it? We did sleep together."

His bluntness surprised her, and she looked embarrassed. He reached over and took her hand. "Was your husband a jerk?"

She shook her head. "No. He's a decent guy. My pregnancy happened sooner than we planned. I was on an antibiotic and birth control failed. But we both did want children. We wanted *this* child. After the miscarriage, he accused me of never putting him first. He accused me of never wanting the baby."

"I haven't known you that long and I know that couldn't be true."

The look in Kaitlyn's eyes was pure vulnerability,

and he wondered if *anyone* really understood her, if she let anyone really know her.

She shook her head and said in a low voice, "To this day, I don't know if the miscarriage was my fault. Did I not want to see the signs? Was that even possible?"

Sitting around the corner from her, he didn't think twice about dropping his arm around her shoulders, about pulling her closer...about bending his head and kissing her.

Oh, he didn't take it too far. After all, they were in a public coffee shop. But he took it far enough—far enough that she knew he wanted to make love with her again...far enough to show her he might already know her better than her husband ever had.

On Tuesday morning, Adam emerged from under Marissa's sink, feeling victorious. "You're good to go. You just needed a new shutoff valve."

Marissa had watched Erica, along with Jordan, while he'd driven to the hardware store to gather everything he'd need. It had been an easy fix.

"Is there a reason you didn't call the landlord?" he asked, curious.

"Yep. It would have taken two weeks for him to get someone here. My kitchen would have been underwater till then."

Marissa's apartment was charming because of the way she'd decorated it and cared for it, but it was definitely worn around the edges. He could tell the landlord didn't do much with the outside, either.

"How about a piece of chocolate cake?" Marissa offered. "Jase gave me the morning off so you could fix this. I baked it to take some to him and Sara, but there's plenty left."

"I skipped breakfast. Chocolate cake sounds good."

"I have a pot of coffee brewing to go with it."

Jordan sat in a corner of the kitchen, happily playing with pots from the lower cupboard. He banged two lids together.

Startled, Erica gave a little cry from her car seat, but then she settled again.

"I probably keep my place too quiet when she's sleeping," Adam decided.

"I did that with Jordan, too. Sugar and milk with your coffee?"

"Nope. I take it straight."

She laughed, and her pretty black curls bobbed around her face. Adam hadn't been around Marissa much, but he liked her. Still, he didn't feel the sparks of attraction as he did with Kaitlyn. As he sat at Marissa's small table for two, she cut a piece of cake large enough to feed two people and set it in front of him.

"This single parent thing is tough," he said just to make conversation.

"It certainly is. I don't know what I would have done without The Mommy Club."

"You don't have family?"

"No. My mom passed on two years ago. I never expected to get pregnant," she said honestly with a little shrug.

"The dad's out of the picture?"

"Way out of the picture. He doesn't even know about Jordan."

Adam wasn't sure what to say to that. If he fathered a child, he'd certainly want to know about him or her.

She must have seen his dilemma, because she said, "It's complicated. He has a life that doesn't include roots. He left town before I even knew I was pregnant."

"And he hasn't been back?"

She hesitated a moment and then explained, "Rodeo circuit."

Adam certainly didn't know anything about that, yet he suspected a cowboy on the circuit was on the road most of the year.

"So how did The Mommy Club help you? From what I've seen, it's mostly a network."

"Exactly. The first thing they did was help me find a job so I had insurance benefits. That's when Jase hired me. I was living in a boarding house at the time, and they helped find me this apartment. After Jordan was born, I went to a workshop for new parents and that's how I met Kaitlyn. She's absolutely super. And the free clinic she's helping with next week will benefit a lot of moms and kids. Dads and kids, too, I guess."

He smiled. "I think this might be a little easier for women. I'm not sure why."

"I don't know about easier," she responded. "Maybe we talk to each other more. The truth is, I'd rather do it alone and have a network like The Mommy Club than always wonder if a man is going to stay."

He wondered if that was a fear of Kaitlyn's, too. She knew he wasn't going to stay, and that was preventing them from having an…affair.

"Do you date?" Adam asked Marissa, wanting to know a little bit about a woman's psyche. If he did, maybe he could understand Kaitlyn and Tina better.

"Nope. I don't have time. I don't even want to think

about it. Flirting with the wrong man led to Jordan's birth."

"Is there any way to know when you've met the *right* man?"

"Since I have a son now to think about, he'd have to have a stable life. He'd have to have the same dreams I have. Children *do* change everything. Have you heard from your sister?"

"Once. I call and give her progress reports every day."

"She's probably scared to come home, scared she won't be enough for her little girl. I can relate to that," Marissa said, looking down at Erica and over at Jordan.

So the question was—just how could he allay some of Tina's fears? Maybe he couldn't, but maybe Kaitlyn could. Maybe if Kaitlyn left a message for Tina, Tina would understand she'd have a support system when she got back.

He'd ask Kaitlyn this afternoon after he watched her tape her interview.

Chapter Nine

On Tuesday afternoon, as the TV production tech made final adjustments to the microphone on her lapel, Kaitlyn kept her eyes on Adam as he held Erica in her baby sling. He was standing just outside the periphery of the activity on a back patio at Raintree Winery, a tall, broad-shouldered reminder that she had plenty of moral support. He was more than moral support really. He was…

He was sexy and determined and gentle and caring. Kaitlyn realized there was a strong connection between them, one that grown deeper ever since they'd made love almost two weeks ago.

Suddenly a woman who looked to be in her thirties was standing before her, extending her hand. "Hello, Dr. Foster, I'm Tanya Edwards. We spoke on the phone."

Yes, they had. Since she'd agreed to this interview, Kaitlyn had heard Tanya Edwards liked to go deep into personal questioning and that made her a little nervous. But this was for a good cause. If telling her story helped more Mommy Club organizations begin in small towns everywhere, life could be so much better for so many families.

Five minutes later, Kaitlyn and Tanya were seated on the patio facing each other, cameras rolling. The opening questions were easy ones to discuss.

"Tell me a little bit about The Mommy Club, the organization you're involved with in Fawn Grove."

Kaitlyn did so with alacrity. Her gaze met Adam's at one point and he gave her a thumbs-up sign. She smiled back and Tanya caught it.

"Jase Cramer, the Pulitzer award-winning photojournalist, has written a series of articles about The Mommy Club and the women it has helped. But you chose to write your own account of what the organization means to you. Why was that?"

"I wanted my article to act as a letter to all the women out there who had been in a position like mine."

"And tell us exactly what that position was."

Kaitlyn had written her article like a blog, and it had felt therapeutic at the time. But answering questions like this, with the cameras rolling, knowing a public greater than Fawn Grove was going to view her and hear her, was suddenly disconcerting.

Still, she answered the question without giving away much emotion. "I was married, pregnant and had so many dreams about a family. But suddenly everything went wrong. I had preeclampsia and didn't realize it. I had a miscarriage."

"I'm so sorry," Tanya said, obviously meaning it. "As you said, only women in your position would understand exactly what you went through. And you could understand what they went through. Is that right?"

"That's true now. That's one of the gifts The Mommy Club gave me. After..." She hesitated. "I had my profession to keep me focused. But going to my practice day after day and seeing children was difficult when I'd wanted one of my own. So I joined a support group through The Mommy Club organization. That helped me get my emotional life back on track."

"Losing the baby, of course, threw it off track," the interviewer said, again with empathy. "I can certainly understand that. But then, you lost something else, didn't you?"

For whatever reason, Kaitlyn was tense now, not wanting to go into all of this...her marriage and divorce. But she plunged ahead to get it over with.

"Yes, I lost my marriage, too. After the miscarriage, everything just seemed to fall apart."

"You and your husband didn't attend counseling together or seek support?"

"At the time we weren't sure where to turn. I wanted to—" She stopped.

"Are you saying your husband had no desire to go to counseling with you?" the reporter asked, digging deeper.

How had she gotten into *this*? Somehow, she had to be diplomatic as well as honest. "Losing a baby is a traumatic time. I don't know if either of us was thinking clearly."

"So your husband didn't want to go to counseling, but you did, and you grew apart. Maybe cracks that had been in the marriage all along seemed even bigger?"

That had certainly been the case. But this time, Kaitlyn didn't answer, and Tanya Edwards saw that she wouldn't.

So she continued with, "Dr. Foster, let me ask you this. Since you *are* a doctor, did your husband blame you for the miscarriage?"

Kaitlyn had already told Adam that she knew Tom blamed her. He blamed her for more than the miscarriage. He blamed her for not seeing the signs. He blamed her for not being the woman he'd expected her to be. And she blamed him, for being nonreactive, for being cold, for being matter-of-fact when he should have held her in his arms and cried with her. To Kaitlyn's dismay, she felt tears prick in her eyes now and her throat practically closed.

Tanya laid her hand on Kaitlyn's. "Take your time, Dr. Foster, I know this is difficult."

"It's past," Kaitlyn said, swallowing hard.

"The experience might be past, but your feelings obviously aren't. Maybe what's keeping them alive is the way you still feel about your ex-husband."

Kaitlyn was stumped and stunned. If she said she felt nothing for her ex-husband, that wouldn't be the truth. She and Tom weren't enemies, though at the end they'd been barely civil. They'd had good times. No, they hadn't had the burning love star-crossed lovers are made of, but they'd had affection and companionship and—

All the excuses in the world couldn't make up for their broken marriage. All the help in the world couldn't have put it back together again. Not if Tom was going to blame her for the rest of his life for what had happened. She could accept his blame because she'd blamed herself, too.

She still did.

She reached for the glass of water sitting on the table by her elbow. Her hand was shaky as she lifted it to her lips. When she brought her gaze up to the crowd, not only the interviewer was watching her, but so were Adam, Sara and Jase. They were watching her lose her composure. She *never* lost her composure. It was the protection that kept her stiff-lipped and firmhearted. But today, something had happened.

Somehow Kaitlyn finished the rest of the interview, driving the crux of it into her practice now, and how that played into The Mommy Club.

"I'm on call for them. The day care run by The Mommy Club has volunteers who call me when they have a sick child or a crisis. With my hospital rounds, my practice, my home visits and other Mommy Club volunteer work, I don't have time to dwell on the past. I move forward each day, helping any way I can. I want to extend an invitation to everyone who's listening. Get involved in your community. Become a part of some organization that makes you realize you're not alone. If you're not alone, others aren't, either."

The interviewer wrapped up the interview with an ease that told Kaitlyn she had done it many times before.

As the tech divested Kaitlyn of her mike, her heart was still beating way too fast, and she felt trembly from the emotions that had been excavated…that she'd thought had been put to rest long ago.

Adam came up to her, but he didn't have Erica now.

"Sara says she'll watch Erica this evening. I'll drive you back to your place."

"I'm fine, Adam. Really," she said brightly.

Adam held his knuckle under the tip of her chin and looked deeply into her eyes. "Now, without that fake steel in your voice, tell me that you're fine."

Maybe it was that she'd had to face too much honesty today. Maybe it was the fact that since Adam had arrived in her life, she'd had to face too much honesty altogether.

Whichever it was, she just didn't feel like she could spar with him right now.

"I'm not going to collapse or cry because of an interview."

"Of course you're not. Do you still go to that Mommy Club group?"

"No. I stopped about a year ago."

He arched his brows. "My point exactly. Come on, we can order a pizza and relax at your place."

Kaitlyn didn't feel like fighting him…and maybe she *did* want to feel his strong arms around her, holding her close.

Adam liked Kaitlyn's place as soon as he walked in. The couch was blue and yellow flowers, and the pattern was repeated on a valance above a huge picture window. The living room was filled with natural light, and Adam was suddenly struck by the fact that that's what Kaitlyn brought with her whenever she entered a room. She brought clarity and helped so many people.

Right now, however, he felt she needed a little clarity herself. Maybe he did, too. She'd told him her husband was a good guy. She obviously hadn't wanted to spill the beans in that interview. Though she wouldn't admit it, *was* she still in love with him? Did she have the hope of getting back together with him? Was that why she couldn't let herself fall into passion?

His gaze returned to her living quarters. There was a huge, comfy cream leather chair with a giant ottoman. Arranged on either side of the couch were stained-glass lamps fashioned in jewel colors.

But more than the furnishings, he was struck by the mementos, the kinds of things he didn't have in his condo. He spotted a photograph of her with Marissa and Jordan, and another with her, Sara, Jase and Amy. On the wall, there was a grouping where a very young Kaitlyn stood with her arms around what he imagined were her parents. Those photos were surrounded by others of the ocean and he wondered if that was a favorite place she used to go with them. She didn't talk about her parents and he wondered if that was because she missed them, or because there was something else there that hurt.

The question for him was—why did he care about all these details?

"How about some iced tea?" she asked brightly… a little too brightly. "It's peach, no caffeine. I use that when I just want to chill."

Chilling was fine, but when she looked at him and their gazes met, there was no chill in the air. In fact, he saw heat rise to her cheeks, and he felt that thumping awareness that he just couldn't escape around her.

"Or, I have wine," she said. "I'm definitely covered tonight."

She'd been covered the first night they met, too. That's why she'd allowed herself the wine tasting.

"Raintree Wine?" he guessed.

"What else? This one's my favorite, though."

"That's fine. Need help?"

"I can handle it."

She must have realized how self-sufficient she sounded because she added, "But I always admire a man who knows how to use a corkscrew."

He laughed. "Bring it on."

Her kitchen picked up the yellow and cream from the living room. The upper cupboards were cream with country flair. The lower cupboards were darker, and he liked the mix. Everything about Kaitlyn shouted good taste—what she wore, what she said, where she lived, what she did. But that wasn't why he liked her. He just…liked her…lusted after her…dreamed about hours in bed with her with his arms wrapped around her.

After a glance at him when their eyes met and time and place seemed to drop away, she broke eye contact and opened an upper cupboard.

"I have a favor to ask."

She glanced at him. "Sure. What?" She seemed eager to talk about anything other than the interview.

"Could you give Tina a call and leave her a message about The Mommy Club? I think it would help, hearing someone else say it."

She nodded. "Of course. I'd be glad to. I can explain I'm looking out for Erica, too, as a pediatrician. I can emphasize all the ways The Mommy Club can help her if she comes back. She wouldn't be alone."

"Thank you," Adam said, meaning it.

Their gazes met. Again Kaitlyn looked away.

She stretched to reach wineglasses on the highest shelf of the cupboard.

"Don't use them much?" he asked lightly.

"Not the good ones. These were my mom's."

If that wasn't an opening, he'd never heard one. He didn't know how to ask it, so he just asked, "Is your mom still living?"

"No. She passed away before I earned my medical degree."

"Something serious? Not that anything isn't serious if it takes your life."

"It was pancreatic cancer. That's a silent killer because there aren't symptoms until it's too late."

"I'm sorry."

He meant it because he knew what it was like to grow up without a mother. "How about your dad?"

"My mom and dad divorced when I was ten. He fell in love with someone else. At first he called on my birthday and that kind of thing, but then he and his wife had a baby and then another. He's very happy and living in Portland."

Now Adam understood better Kaitlyn's need for stability and a future. Her father had left. Her husband had left. As an adult, she'd had no one to depend on but herself. That formed a very clear picture of why Kaitlyn was the person she was.

The crystal wineglasses she poured the wine into were beautiful.

"Hand wash only?" he asked, as they carried their glasses into the living room.

"Almost all delicate things need extra care."

"Like hearts." Now where had that come from? He'd never been considered poetic in his life.

As they sank down on the sofa together, they were thigh to thigh, knee to knee, but neither of them moved away. Kaitlyn was wearing a flowered dress, not too professional, not too casual. It was just right for that interview. He'd worn khakis and a tan oxford shirt. With taking care of Erica, he wasn't thinking much about clothes these days. He just grabbed something, like when he was on a site in a foreign country.

They'd taken a couple of sips of wine when he decided just to jump right in.

"So how do you think the interview went?"

Kaitlyn didn't answer right away, but took a few more sips of wine.

"Kaitlyn?"

When she looked at him then, he saw that vulnerability again in her eyes that he wanted to kiss away.

"I was prepared for it. After all, I wrote about everything we were going to talk about. But the way she asked those questions—" Kaitlyn shook her head. "She got to me. She made me feel things I thought I was done with. Memories came rushing back, both good and bad."

He put his wineglass down and hung his arm around her shoulders, taking her back with him against the sofa cushions. "The older you get, the more potent memories become. Bittersweet, too. Tell me something. Do you regret your divorce?"

"As I said before, I regret that our marriage didn't work."

"I admire the way you answered the questions. You were honest and sincere and that came across. Ms. Edwards should be nothing but satisfied with that interview, and so should you."

After a long pause, Kaitlyn said, "I appreciated you being there."

The way she was looking up at him, and the way he was feeling, there was no way that he couldn't bend his head and kiss her. They were alone. *Really* alone. No baby in the next room. No cell phone beeping. Nothing to interrupt them. He wanted her and he wanted her badly.

As if she'd finally relaxed, as if she'd realized the interview was over and she could let her guard down again, she wrapped her arms around his neck and leaned into him. It was easy to scoop her onto his lap, easy to kiss her deeply, easy to take passion further.

Their kiss invited passion in. It invited them to explore, to enjoy each other, to revel in every sensation, every breath, every touch. When his hand cupped her breast, she pushed toward it, seemingly eager for more. Yet after what had transpired at the interview, after their conversation in the kitchen, Adam knew he had to stop and ask a question.

He broke off the kiss, cupped her face between his hands, and asked, "Is this what you want?"

She looked dazed, as if she'd been somewhere she didn't want to return from. But then her focus returned, and she shook her head a little. "When I'm with you, my needs and wants get all confused," she admitted.

"I shouldn't have started this."

"It started that night at the winery."

She was so right about that. The chemistry between them couldn't be denied. But somehow they had to control it. Somehow they had to keep their hearts safe in the midst of their desire.

"I want you," Adam said. "But I want *now* and you want forever. Those two don't mix."

"There rarely is a compromise," she murmured. "Nobody wants to give in or give up."

She was talking from marriage experience again, something he knew nothing about. Except he had seen that same concept played over and over again with Jade and his father. Maybe marriage really was an illusion that could never live up to reality. Maybe he should just forget about Dr. Kaitlyn Foster and concentrate on finding his sister.

It was midmorning the next day when Kaitlyn walked into an exam room and found Marissa with Jordan. The little boy giggled when he saw her and raised his arms.

Being a friend, as well as the little boy's doctor, was an advantage. He was here for a well-baby checkup and it should be a breeze, since he wasn't afraid of her. So many children came to the doctor afraid, and she had to put them at ease.

As she gave Jordan a hug, she smiled at Marissa. "Thanks for coming to the interview taping. We haven't really talked, though, since the bachelor auction. How did we do?"

"We did great! Thirty thousand dollars to put in

The Mommy Club fund. I wish I knew who receives it when I send it to that P.O. Box address in San Jose."

"I guess that's part of the mystique of The Mommy Club. No one knows all there is to know."

"Speaking of the bachelor auction, how did it go while you babysat for Adam and he had a date?"

Kaitlyn took her stethoscope with its cartoon-character cover and let Jordan hold it. "Erica's a good baby. She slept most of the time."

"I wasn't talking about Erica."

"Adam wasn't out real late."

"You knew about Sherry Conniff, didn't you?"

"Adam told me." She took the stethoscope from Jordan's hand, tickled his tummy and put the ends of it in her ears.

"I'm going to lift your shirt up," she told him. "We're going to play a little game of 'Listen to Your Heart.' I'll let you listen, too, okay?"

All was quiet while she did just that, and he actually sat still for her. But then he got fidgety and she tapped the appliquéd dog on his pants.

"Woof, woof," she said, making it as realistic as she could.

"Woof," he repeated as best he could.

As Kaitlyn let Jordan listen to his heart, his eyes became wide and he grinned at her.

"Adam seemed supportive at the interview," Marissa prompted.

Last evening after their kiss, they'd ordered pizza and pretended to be just friends. Adam had left without kissing her good-night.

But they weren't just friends.

Kaitlyn could be honest with Marissa. "I don't

know why, but that interview opened up wounds I thought were healed."

"Maybe that's because you don't think about them or talk about them."

Kaitlyn's gaze met Marissa's.

"You don't talk about *your* history, either. You've been through a lot, too. Having a baby alone is no picnic."

"At first I felt as if my world crashed in. One night leads to a pregnancy. *I* didn't even know about it when he left."

"Will you ever tell him?"

"I doubt it. There's simply no reason for me to contact him because he doesn't *want* to be a father."

"What if he ever comes back?"

"He won't. He wants the life he has, and the last thing I'd ever want to do is trap someone into staying with me...or caring for a child."

Marissa studied Kaitlyn. "But this conversation is supposed to be about you and Adam. He's leaving in a few weeks, isn't he?"

"That's what he plans to do."

"What about Erica?"

"I don't think he's faced that decision yet, especially since Tina called him. He's hopeful she'll come back. And he might be right."

"But Adam will be back. He returns to Fawn Grove between assignments."

"Yes, he does. But what kind of relationship would that be?"

"I suppose it depends on what kind of relationship you want. Have you fallen for him?"

Yes, she had. She might as well admit that to herself. She was in love with Adam Preston and she didn't know what she was going to do about it.

Chapter Ten

Kaitlyn didn't know if she was doing the right thing or not, but she couldn't stop thinking about Adam and everything they'd shared in the short time she'd known him. Maybe time didn't make any difference at all. Maybe for a change she should follow her heart instead of her head. But did she even know how?

Her interview would be airing tonight. She and Marissa and Sara were going to watch it together at Raintree. She was excited about it yet still a little nervous. She wanted to be a good representative for The Mommy Club. She wanted to inspire other towns to open chapters of the organization.

But that wasn't why she was standing in her office, staring at her phone, considering what she was going to do about Adam. She still had notes to make on charts before joining Marissa and Sara at Raintree.

She wasn't worried about getting those done before she left, but she was worried about this phone call. Was it the right thing to do?

Was there really a right thing or a wrong thing in this situation?

She picked up the phone and dialed. He might not even pick up if he was feeding Erica or getting himself supper—

But he did pick up. "Hi, Kaitlyn. Did you call to remind me to watch tonight?"

She had to smile. "Obviously you remembered so I don't have to."

He laughed. "True. Besides, what else do I have to do once Erica's asleep for the night, or asleep for four hours, which is her routine now."

"I'm sure if you wanted to find a babysitter and do something else, you could."

"Yes, I could, but I'm not. I do have an appointment tomorrow with that private eye I told you about. Mary's going to watch Erica again."

"Is he in Fawn Grove?"

"No, he's in Sacramento." There was a pause until he asked, "Is there another reason you called?"

She inhaled a very deep breath. "Actually there is. After rounds, tomorrow's my day off. I'm going to go grocery shopping. So I was wondering if you and Erica would like to come over for dinner."

Her pulse was suddenly beating a lot faster, and she was actually holding her breath waiting for his answer. One second passed…then two.

Finally, he responded, "I certainly won't turn down the opportunity for a home-cooked meal. My sunny-side-up eggs for dinner don't exactly qualify."

So he was coming for the *food?* If so, she might as well ask, "So what's your favorite dinner?"

"I'm not picky. I usually have to catch something on the run, and when I'm in a foreign country, I never know what will turn up on my plate."

She could go all out. She could make his mouth water. For more than food? Possibly. But they'd start with that.

"How about beef tenderloin, baby asparagus, garlic smashed potatoes? And for dessert, apple dumplings. My mom taught me how to make really good ones."

"Are you sure you want to go to all that trouble?"

She was sure. But she was going to have to play it by ear, keep her head and use the dinner conversation to figure out where Adam stood in their relationship, if they even *had* a relationship. Maybe that's what she wanted to figure out most. Maybe she was just infatuated with him. Maybe she didn't really love him.

One dinner wouldn't give her all the answers, but it might give her a few.

"I'm sure I want to make you dinner. I appreciated you coming to the interview."

"So this is payback?"

Now *she'd* gotten boxed into a corner. "Not exactly. Maybe we can talk about that."

"Talk about payback?"

"Adam—"

"I'll bring along Erica's swing and her portable crib. Hopefully she won't have a fussy spell that lasts three hours."

"If she does, we'll deal with it."

"That's the great thing about dating a pediatrician. This is a date, isn't it?"

His husky question touched her heart, and she couldn't play games with him. "I'd like to think of it that way."

"What time do you want me there?"

"How about seven?"

"Seven, it is. You *are* recording the interview, aren't you? We can always play back the best parts."

This time she laughed. "I think we can find better things to do than that."

"I'm sure we can." That sounded like a husky promise.

When Adam walked into Kaitlyn's town house with Erica the following evening, he was struck by so many things at once. The good smells of cooking filled the rooms. Besides that, she'd set a fresh bouquet of flowers on the marble-topped table in the small foyer. Toys Erica could play with, with a little help, lay on the coffee table—a rattle, a teething key and a stuffed turtle.

All of it together made him feel as if…as if he had a hole in his heart. He couldn't remember much about his childhood home, maybe because after his mother died, everything had turned to black and white. His dad had sold the house and moved into an apartment so someone else would do the cleaning and gardening and handle the upkeep. That was the case until his father had married Jade. Then they'd all moved into a house together until Jade and his dad had divorced. The house had seemed empty after Tina and her mother had moved out. After Adam went off to college, his dad had again moved into an apartment.

Oddly, Kaitlyn's place felt like a home. The feeling unsettled him. Was it the place? Or was it Kaitlyn?

Because there she stood with an apron tied over her green sweater and slacks. She looked delicious, and he wanted to run his hands through her hair and take her into his arms.

However, Erica wasn't happy the car had stopped moving and that he'd carried her inside. She was wiggling around and screwing up her little face and turning red. Crying would come next.

"Uh-oh," Kaitlyn said. "Did she wake up when the car stopped?"

"Almost. She's waking up now."

Kaitlyn unbuckled the harness in the car seat and scooped Erica into her arms. "Oh, no, you don't, baby. There's no need to fuss. Sooner than you can wave that little hand in the air, Uncle Adam is going to have your swing set up."

He laughed. "I'm good, but I don't know if I'm that fast. Do you have to keep your eye on dinner or can you walk her a little?"

"I can walk her. I'll take her out on the patio."

As he put the swing together, Adam watched Kaitlyn with Erica. This time, that hole in his heart seemed to grow even deeper. What was wrong with him tonight?

Kaitlyn was standing on the patio holding the baby in her arms and staring up at the mountains in the distance as Adam went outside. There was something so elementally right about the tableau. He wondered if *he* looked right when he was holding Erica, if being a dad to her wasn't so far-fetched. He couldn't let anything happen to her. He had to watch over her.

When the back door closed, Kaitlyn didn't turn around.

He crossed to her and stood close beside her. "She settled down?"

"She likes the view."

"I think *you* like the view."

Kaitlyn nodded. "I'd love to have a house near Raintree Winery, sort of in the foothills of the mountains. The peace and quiet would be wonderful after a day at the office or at the hospital."

"And you plan to make that happen." He could hear the determination in her voice.

"Someday." She looked up at him then. "How did your meeting go?"

"I like the P.I. He made sense in a lot of ways. He says if Tina's still using her actual phone to call me, and it seemed that she was, that's a good indication she wants to be found, or that she's coming back. But he said he'll do some investigating for me and let me know what he finds out. He has a reputation for being discreet so I'm not concerned about that."

"What *are* you concerned about?"

"That when she finds out I put a P.I. on her trail, she'll think I don't trust her."

"*Do* you trust her?"

"I don't know her that well anymore. That's the crux of it. But that's more to do with me than with her."

After a few moments, she said, "I called Tina. I hope my message helps."

They stood together, shoulders brushing, staring at the beautiful view.

"Are you hungry?" she asked.

Now he made eye contact and responded, "Very hungry."

"Then I'd better get those potatoes smashed and steam the asparagus."

If he bent to her now and kissed her, the whole night might take a different course. But she was holding Erica and now didn't seem the time to let his desire catch fire. "I set up her swing in the kitchen. I'll see if I can get her settled in it."

"By the time you do that, the meat will be ready to carve. Do you want to give it a try?"

Adam remembered the pretense of Thanksgivings with a housekeeper bringing the turkey to the table. His dad had botched carving every way he could. Tina and Adam hadn't cared because they were all together as a family. But then there was the Thanksgiving before the split up, and then the Thanksgiving after the split up. Then there was no turkey to carve, no family to ask over. They were separate families with separate fears.

Kaitlyn must have been a mind reader because she asked, "What kind of celebration are you going to have for Thanksgiving this year? It's not far off."

"That all depends on where I've been, or where I still am. Thanksgiving won't mean much if I'm in the middle of a desert, or if Tina's not home."

"Adam, what happens if Tina doesn't come home? What happens with Erica, I mean?"

"I guess I'll become her dad," he said with a certainty he hadn't felt before.

"And your work?"

"I would have to figure that out somehow. When I left Tina a message yesterday about Erica, I told her the date I have to leave for Thailand. I'm hoping that will bring her to her senses."

Kaitlyn gave him a long look and then a little nod. He wondered if she thought he *could* be a dad. He wondered the same thing.

Erica happily cooed and gooed in her swing as they ate dinner and didn't talk about anything serious. He found there was always so much to talk about with Kaitlyn, even though her life was filled with her practice and medical journals. The Mommy Club kept her informed about so many other issues. They both seemed to be enjoying their conversation, as if it were a prelude to something else, as if maybe Kaitlyn would give in to desire and pleasure and the moment.

Their hands touched as they reached for a serving dish at the same time. When their gazes met, Adam felt that little rock in his world that always surprised him. Kaitlyn looked a bit startled, too. Their shoulders easily bumped with their close proximity.

She had a tiny smear of butter on her upper lip. He leaned in and kissed it away. He didn't do more than that. When he leaned back, she looked as if she wanted more. Good. Later there would be more.

Recovering her composure, Kaitlyn dished out the dessert. The apple dumpling was everything an apple dumpling should be—cinnamon, sugar, walnuts and a flaky dough that just fell apart...or melted in your mouth.

"You should sell these. You'd make a fortune," Adam joked.

"I could never make them in quantity. I guess a little bit of love goes into each one as I remember my mom."

They gazed deeply into each other's eyes.

"Thank you for this dinner," he said. He was going

to say more. He was going to do more, like maybe kiss her again...when the doorbell rang twice in succession.

"Are you expecting anyone?" he asked.

She looked puzzled. "No." Pushing her chair back, she stood. "It could be Marissa or Sara. I'll see."

Not that Adam didn't respect or admire Kaitlyn's friendships, but he was hoping it was a pizza guy trying to deliver a pizza to the wrong address.

However, when he heard a raised male voice, he had the suspicion it wasn't the pizza guy.

Checking on Erica and seeing that she looked content, Adam pushed his chair back, stood and went to the doorway where he could overhear what was happening in the living room.

"I talked about you as little as possible in the interview," Kaitlyn maintained.

"You talked about our marriage. Everybody knows I was married to you. You made me sound like a jerk."

So *this* was Tom, Adam surmised.

"I spoke about my miscarriage. The interviewer asked if that led to our divorce. I told her it was part of it. I can't help what conclusions she drew."

"You were just being honest," Tom said sarcastically.

"Yes. As honest as you were being when you asked for a divorce because you blamed me for the death of our baby."

Adam almost took a step forward, concerned old wounds were going to cause more than an argument.

"And you resent me for it. That's why you did the interview," her ex-husband tossed back.

Now Adam *did* step forward. Kaitlyn didn't have to take abuse from her ex.

"Watch your tone," he said with a threat in his voice. Adam stood by Kaitlyn's shoulder and could see the apparent surprise on her ex-husband's face.

Suddenly from the kitchen, Erica began crying. A baby's world wasn't much different from an adult's. One moment content, the next in an upheaval.

Tom looked into the kitchen, saw the swing with Erica and a shadow crossed his face. "I thought you'd be…alone," he muttered. "We'll talk sometime when you don't have company. But don't give any more interviews without alerting me first."

As Adam turned to see to Erica, he heard Kaitlyn say, "I don't have to alert you, Tom, not when I'm just telling the truth. But out of courtesy, if I ever do another interview, I will."

Adam didn't hear a goodbye from Tom Foster, but he did hear the door close.

The swing had stopped its motion and that's what Erica seemed upset about. He wound it up again and it started. Within a few seconds, she seemed content.

Kaitlyn looked a little pale when she entered the kitchen.

"Does that happen often?" he wanted to know.

"That hasn't happened ever. I haven't seen him since the divorce."

"So what do you think brought him here tonight?"

"He said it was the interview."

"But you didn't say anything that would paint him as a jerk. Loss divides couples—everybody understands that. Do you think he saw the article in the paper?"

She shook her head. "I don't know. But that was just the Fawn Grove paper. Jase said it was syndicated, but Tom wouldn't know that. The fact that this was TV and a much bigger viewing public must have had something to do with it. He was always very concerned with appearances."

"Does his job depend upon them?"

"Partly. He's in marketing. He has to make contacts and keep contacts and make sure they think highly of him. But I never thought an interview like this would have any effect on him."

Adam pulled out the kitchen chair and said to Kaitlyn, "Sit down. You look a little shell-shocked. I'll pour you more iced tea."

"Adam, you don't have to get me anything."

"Don't argue with me, Kaitlyn. Just tell me what you want."

When she looked at him, with those beautiful green eyes, he saw more than he wanted to see. She wouldn't tell him exactly what she wanted because it was far beyond his ken. She kept it simple.

"Tea would be good."

"He sounds like he always wants to be right," Adam commented as he went to the refrigerator.

"*Everybody* wants to be right. At the beginning, he was attentive and charming and supportive. But being involved with a doctor isn't easy. I think he became resentful of so many things."

"Would you do another interview if one came up?"

"It depends on the cause."

"He ambushed you. Did he do that often when you were married?"

It was several beats before she answered. "Now

that you mention it, maybe he did. I never considered that as a strategy, but when he wanted to confront me about something, it was always when I'd just come home from work, or just finished rounds at the hospital, or even on my way to a meeting. That's when he'd pounce to tell me about a new idea or something we should be doing differently."

"And you didn't catch on until—"

"Until I got the divorce. At the beginning of our marriage, Tom and I had normal conversations, just like anyone does. But the busier we got, the less time we had, so every conversation was on the run. Maybe that's why some of them seemed like an ambush."

"Maybe if Erica and I hadn't been here tonight, you could have settled things."

"There's nothing to settle. I doubt if there will ever be another interview. But if there is, I'll let him know."

"I think he wanted to talk to you, Kaitlyn, really talk to you. He might have regrets. I think *you* do."

"Being involved with a doctor isn't easy," she said again. "My hours were sporadic even after I joined the practice."

"You had a career. He had a career. You have to stop making excuses for him. Maybe you *do* still have feelings for him."

"I still have feelings about the dreams that never materialized and the baby we lost. But I don't have feelings and dreams about *him*. Adam, you've got to believe that."

Did he? After seeing what had happened here tonight, he wasn't sure Kaitlyn was over her ex-husband, or whether her ex was over her.

"Are you going to talk to him again?"

"I'll see if he calls."

"I know you, Kaitlyn. You like everything settled in a box. If he doesn't call you, you'll call him."

Silence pervaded the kitchen after that comment. They didn't talk as they cleaned up the kitchen together.

Once Adam started the dishwasher, he said, "It's getting near Erica's bedtime. I can feed her and try to get her to fall asleep in the crib, but it could take a while."

Kaitlyn looked troubled, and Adam didn't want to start anything that would mix up her feelings even further. When a woman dreamed of white picket fences and tomorrow, and she'd lost that dream, sometimes she wanted to hold on to it even harder. On the other hand, some disappointed women would just settle for what they could get.

He didn't like that thought, not at all. Because settling for the kind of passion they had wasn't settling, it was exploring. It was taking that roller-coaster ride, and it was remaining free and simply enjoying each other.

But as Kaitlyn stopped by Erica's swing, as she paced around the kitchen, as she moved the coffee canister to the left and then to the right, he knew tonight wasn't going to be about exploring or enjoying.

He went to her and wrapped his arms around her. "What can I do?"

She shook her head. "I wish I knew. I wish I knew why Tom's visit upset me so much."

"The pain is still there," Adam told her. "You're trying to make it go away by moving forward. Maybe he buried it, and the interview excavated it. It could be as simple as that. But I do think you have to explore what you had and what you might still want, maybe with him."

She looked as if she were about to protest, but then she stopped. "After the divorce, I shut off all my feelings toward him. I was angry he had asked for the divorce. I was angry he blamed me. I was most angry that he even wouldn't try to work it out."

"So you didn't want to give up."

"It's a bad habit of mine. I don't like to fail."

There was a difference, however, between not wanting to fail and still being in love with a man.

With his arm around her, he tilted her close and gave her a kiss that was meant to be consoling. But as with any time they kissed, rockets went off and the explosions rattled them. They tore apart.

"You want to think about all of it," he said reasonably.

"And you don't understand why I have to."

"Oh, I understand why you have to. I just don't like where it might be headed."

"I don't like where *you* might be headed."

Stalemate. Again.

He wouldn't be making love to Kaitlyn Foster tonight. They'd be in their separate residences, doing their separate things.

Suddenly, being separate didn't seem freeing to him at all.

An hour later, with one arm around Erica's car seat with her in it, Adam slipped his key into its lock, ready to feed his niece and then hopefully settle her for the night. At least for a few hours of it. But he found the lock already open.

At first he just stood there, clicking through his head the number of people who had a key to his condo. The manager, of course, his father, Tina— Maybe Tina had come for Erica.

However, when he pushed the door open and stepped inside, he saw his father. George Preston lay on the sofa, his legs stretched out before him, the TV blaring with the remote on his chest.

"Dad. What are you doing here?"

His father sat up and shrugged. "Waiting for you. Where have you been?"

Erica must have already caught the tension in the air, because she was wiggling in her car seat, getting ready to wail at a high decibel.

Trying to avert the inevitable, he set her on the armchair, quickly unfastened the harness and lifted her out. "I was having dinner with…a friend."

"It couldn't have been much of a date with a baby along," his father said wryly, swinging his legs to the floor. He came over to Adam, narrowed his eyes and stared at his grandchild.

"Little thing, isn't she?"

"She's only ten weeks old."

"There's not much hair, either."

Adam felt affronted for his niece. "This is a stage babies go through. She'll grow more hair, and it will probably be thick and silky like Tina's."

"Unless the daddy was bald," his father joked.

Adam wasn't in the mood for jokes. "Really, Dad, why are you here? Did Tina contact you?" That was possible, he supposed.

"No, she didn't contact me. But you laid a guilt trip on me when we talked. After all, I *was* Tina's stepfather for a short time."

"You still *are* her stepfather." Adam wanted to make it clear the responsibility didn't end when a marriage broke up, not when children were involved.

"So I'm here now. Have you heard from her?"

Did his father really want to help find Tina, or did he have another agenda?

"She called. I leave a message on her phone every day. But I've also hired a P.I. to do some investigating. I want to find her sooner rather than later."

Erica began to cry. She was probably hungry and Adam wasn't fulfilling her needs.

"A P.I.? That will cost a pretty penny. I understand you want to get the baby out of your life, but—"

"I do *not* want to get the baby out of my life," Adam protested. His vehemence surprised even himself.

His father studied him. "What's come over you?"

"Look, Dad, if you came to help, that's great. Do you want to take turns babysitting Erica?"

His father looked disgusted. "Get reasonable, Adam. I don't know anything about taking care of a baby."

"I didn't, either, but I learned quick."

"I brought someone with me."

Adam looked around as if he'd missed someone when he walked in. "Who?"

"Iris. And I'm going to marry her. I thought maybe you'd like to meet her. We're going to fly to Las Vegas day after tomorrow."

His father was trying to talk above Erica's cries, and his voice kept rising higher and higher, along with hers. At least all the noise gave Adam time to think. It gave him time to realize his father was only thinking of himself again.

"If you say you brought this woman with you—"

"Iris," his father reminded him.

"Fine, Iris. Where is she?"

"She's staying at a five-star hotel in Sacramento. What did you think I was going to do with her? Throw her into this?"

By "this" he meant Erica's fuss. Annoyed with him, intent on meeting Erica's needs, Adam crossed to the kitchen. With the car seat on the counter, he quickly mixed up a bottle of formula, tested the temperature and then took it with him to the armchair.

As he expertly fed Erica and her cries diminished to contented suckling, he asked his father, "And do you intend to bunk with me?"

"Of course not. I'm staying with Iris. But I did feel a certain responsibility about Tina, and I had to get that settled with you."

"Get what settled?"

"What you're going to do with her baby. After all, if she doesn't return, aren't you going to put her up for adoption?"

Just the thought turned Adam's stomach. Just the thought of giving Erica to anyone else made him feel absolutely sick.

He looked down at the child who'd found a place in his heart. "No, I would *not* put Erica up for adoption, any more than I'd put up a child of mine for adoption. I'm surprised you didn't do that with me after Mom died."

"Adam!"

Had he gone too far? He didn't think so. "Look, Dad, I've had an unusually mixed-up evening. I'm glad you think you've found happiness with Iris. Is she twenty years older than you are, or maybe twenty years younger?"

"Younger," his father snapped. "But that has nothing to do with it."

"Tiffany was twenty years younger than you, too. Anna Mae was fifteen years younger. Do you think these women can give you back your youth?"

His father's brows drew together in an imposing scowl. "Your insolence tonight—"

His father's scowl didn't disturb him anymore. "It's maybe what you need to hear. If you aren't happy with yourself, you'll never be happy with someone else."

"Look who's talking—the man who's never married at all."

Score one for his dad. "Maybe I haven't, but maybe that's because I didn't want to have a marriage like any of yours." He said it sadly without accusation.

"It wasn't my marriages that ruined your life. It was that girl in college. You should have told the police the truth that night."

Adam went perfectly still. When his gaze met his father's, he knew that his dad had known the truth all along. A new respect for his dad came over Adam because his father hadn't been as clueless as he'd thought.

"I loved her and I protected her."

"Love isn't always about protection, Adam. Sometimes it's about telling the truth."

"She has the life she wants."

"And how about you? If you hadn't been charged with reckless driving, if you hadn't been so mixed-up, if you hadn't been rudderless in college, might *your* life have turned out differently?"

Adam thought of Tina and Erica. He thought of the things Sherry had said to him, the bitterness that was now in the past. Then he thought about Kaitlyn.

"Everything in my life has brought me to this point," he responded after some thought. "Now I have to make decisions that are going to affect the rest of it. One of those decisions is what to do about Tina. She needs support, Dad, and I'm not just talking about monetary support. There's an organization here called The Mommy Club. They can help her in so many ways. They can give her a list of the best services with a sliding scale of fees she can afford. They can hook her up with good doctors. They even have a hotline for young mothers who get overwhelmed, as well as affordable day care."

"You learned all this in two short weeks."

"I learned it because I needed to learn it if I was going to take care of Erica. It would be great if you get to know your granddaughter while you're here."

"She's not really—"

"Yes, she is. You married Jade. You were husband and wife. Tina looked to you as her father. You played catch with her. You even drove her to school functions and played board games with her. You became her stepfather during her important years. Certainly you can forget about the possibility of a new wife while you think about that."

Adam's father gave a harrumph, said, "It's a shame I taught you to speak your mind," and picked up his suit coat lying over the sofa. "You get the impression I don't care about Tina. That's not true because I do.

If you need anything, anything at all besides a P.I. to help find her, just let me know and I'll cover the cost."

"I don't think money is going to do it this time, Dad."

"And just what will?"

"Tina knowing that the people she loves will love her back. She ran because we weren't here for her."

"I was in Europe. I was—"

"Those are excuses and I can make the same ones. My job was important. The work I do is important. But more important than my sister? Somehow we got this all wrong, Dad. We're not all separate people, just flying off in a different direction, never connecting again. That's not what family is."

"And what is family, son?" His father suddenly looked as if he had the weight of the world on his shoulders.

Adam's answer came easily. "It's looking into each other's eyes and knowing the other person. It's having memories of them and appreciating them. It's keeping in touch and most of all, keeping tuned in. I wasn't in touch with Tina enough. Yes, she's a big girl, but big girls have bigger problems than little girls. When they have no one to turn to, they get in trouble. She probably didn't even love Erica's father. She probably was lonely and had no one to turn to. Don't you see that's the pattern, Dad? Don't you see that that's what *you* do?"

Instead of the fury Adam expected to see, his father went pensive. "I don't know how to change my ways, Adam, but maybe you're still young enough to change yours. What do you suggest I do about Tina?"

"Call her. Leave a voice mail telling her you love

her. Most of all tell her whether you get married again or not, you'll be glad to spend some time with her and your grandchild when she returns home."

"Adam, you were the last baby I spent any time with. The noise will drive me crazy."

"So get earplugs. I don't care what you do to make this work, Dad, but somehow you have to reassure Tina. You have to show her you haven't forgotten Jade any more than she has."

"You think she misses Jade?"

"Yes, she misses her mother, and I think she misses the backup she always had and doesn't have now. I have a friend who called to assure her that The Mommy Club is here for her. If Tina decides not to come home, then I'll have to make the hard decisions. But not until then. My first goal is to get her home."

"You've changed."

"I had no choice."

But now he saw he had lots of choices, and he wondered which one of those could include Kaitlyn.

Chapter Eleven

It was well after noon on Saturday when Adam stopped at the community center where the free clinic was being held. After his father's visit and especially with the bad taste it had left in his mouth, Adam considered staying away from Kaitlyn. After all, wouldn't that be better for both of them?

On the other hand, his father's visit also prodded him to see Kaitlyn more. Totally crazy. He'd realized his father's way of life wasn't the life he wanted. But what he did want— That was up in the air.

Oh, yes, he wanted Kaitlyn, physically anyway. But then what? Maybe that's what he was trying to figure out.

There were long tables set up for patients' paperwork and screening information. Kaitlyn had told him a few nurses she knew were giving their time, too, today, to help the doctors and make everything go more smoothly. Two pediatricians were participating, as well as two general practitioners. There were four stations set up, one for each doctor. But as Adam looked around, he couldn't find Kaitlyn.

He stopped at one of the reception tables and asked where he might find her.

The middle-aged brunette said, "We made her take her lunch break. She's been seeing patients since 7:00 a.m. All the doctors are taking turns and she was the last one to hold out. We said if she didn't go eat lunch, she couldn't come back in and help anybody. She's in the kitchen area in the back. At least she'd better be," the woman said with a wink.

Adam knew how dedicated Kaitlyn was, and when she saw a need, she wanted to help. Sometimes, maybe, to her own detriment. Trying to make up for losing a child? Possibly. He wished she would stop blaming herself. He wished she could get the old feelings resolved.

Just like you have? a little devil voice inside of him asked.

Right. It was so-o-o easy.

He found Kaitlyn wearing a smock covered with cartoon characters, sitting at a counter, looking through paperwork while she nibbled on a wrap of some kind. Probably something healthy.

But that's why he brought her something *not* quite so healthy. He was hoping he could get her to take a break with him.

Dropping the waxy bag onto a table without making any noise, he came up behind her and suddenly covered her eyes with his hands. "I understand you're supposed to be taking a break."

"Adam!" She turned around right away. "What are you doing here?"

"I figured you'd be having a long day and you'd need some sugar to help you get through it. Actually, there's some protein in it, too."

"What are you talking about?"

"Well, I could have brought Chinese, or Thai, or Italian, but I figured you'd get some kind of lunch here. So instead, I brought these absolutely delicious, sort of like profiteroles. It's a pastry stuffed with mascarpone and peanut butter cream covered in chocolate. Jase and Sara swear by them. A chef they know makes them, and I was able to confiscate a dozen."

He picked up the waxy bag, opened it and set it under her nose. "Take a whiff."

"Adam—"

He gave her a pretend scowl. "The woman out front told me you couldn't practice until you took a break. This is a break. Some kind of healthy chicken wrap isn't. Take a whiff."

Kaitlyn finally smiled. "You can be very convincing."

"*Convincing* is my middle name."

With an askance look at him, she took the bag and inhaled deeply. "They smell divine."

"That's the word Sara used—*divine*. I thought it was a little over-the-top, but what do I know. And, along with this wonderful dessert, I brought you the best hazelnut coffee The Coffee Hut makes. Black, right?"

"Yes, black, and how did you know I liked Coffee Hut coffee?"

"A little bird. Actually, lots of little birds know you like black coffee from The Coffee Hut."

"Everybody in my practice with me, as well as Marissa, Sara, probably Jase and Liam to name just a few. But my big question to you is, why did you go to all this trouble?"

He was beside her at the counter and they were leaning close together. "I didn't like the way we left things the other night."

"Neither did I," she admitted.

"And when I went back to my condo with Erica..."

"Where is Erica?"

"She's with Mary. When I went to the new-parent workshop, she said whenever I need her, I should call her. Serendipitous, don't you think?"

"So we could have this talk?"

"So I could bring you a treat. So I could tell you that I know we both have remnants of the past to clean up." He unfolded the bag, dipped his hand inside, and brought out two of the tasty desserts.

"How hungry are you?" she asked.

For the dessert or for you? that little devil in his head asked him. "I'll tell you what. You take a bite then let me know if you want a whole one, or two or three."

She laughed. "We're not solving anything by eating dessert," she warned him.

"No, we're not. But we're having a damn good time, and since you don't have a whole lot of it, this seemed like a good idea."

He offered her a bite of the chocolate-covered delicacy. She bit into the peanut butter and cheese filling, savoring the chocolate on the outside and getting some on her upper lip. Her tongue came out to swipe it away.

"Oh, my gosh, Adam," she said as she bit in. "I can probably eat a dozen of them and still want more."

He chuckled. "That's what I thought."

Taking a napkin from the bag, he dumped a few onto the napkin and set it in front of her. Then he set her coffee beside it.

"I'm not even going to think about how many calories are in one of these."

"Good. Don't. You don't have to worry about it anyway."

She looked at him as if he'd said something very important. As beautiful as she was, he guessed she might not get many compliments like that. She didn't let herself open to them. Maybe if *he* opened up a little…

"When I got back to my condo Thursday evening, my father was there."

Her eyes widened. "He flew in from England?"

"Apparently. Now don't get the wrong idea. This isn't all about Tina. He brought what could be wife number five—Iris. She's twenty years younger, and he thought maybe I'd like to meet her."

Kaitlyn cautiously took a sip of her coffee. "And what did you say to that?"

"I said I would, but I also told him he'd better be here to let Tina know she still had a dad. He promised to call and leave her a message. Do you think we're bombarding her with too many messages?"

"Not if she needs to know people think about her and care about her."

"Hmm, I thought the same thing. I don't want to push her further into hiding. The P.I. hasn't come up with anything because he thinks she's using cash."

"She has cash?"

"My father sends her checks. I don't think she spends them. She dumps them into a savings account. Just like I did, she has something to prove. She wanted to make it on her own."

"You wanted to do more than make it on your own. You wanted to prove to your father once and for all you didn't need him, and you could become a better man than you thought he was."

She hit *that* on the nose, and he didn't know if he liked it. He let silence invade a conversation that up to now had flowed quite freely.

But after the coffee cups were drained, he asked her, "Have you talked to your ex again?"

"I called him. We're going to have dinner tomorrow to clear the air. I think we both need it."

So she *had* talked to him. So she *had* thought more about what they did and didn't need. Maybe he and Kaitlyn needed to explore what they did and didn't need. There was only one way to find out, one way to nudge them both toward the future.

"What time do you think you'll be finished here?"

"I don't know. It could go late. We don't want to turn any children away."

He wouldn't expect them to. "I keep late hours. When you're finished here, why don't you come over? I'll get some Chinese and we can warm it up."

She was obviously hesitating, and he knew why. A makeshift dinner could lead to a lot more.

"Think about it," he said, rising to his feet. "You can just show up, no call necessary."

"Adam—"

"No pressure, Kaitlyn. No strings on either of us. If you come, you come. If you don't, that's fine, too." But as he said it, he knew that wouldn't be fine at all.

Because he wanted Kaitlyn in his bed, even if he wasn't sure about anything else.

Finished at free clinic for the day, Kaitlyn headed to the parking lot. She drove to her town house, parked, went inside and heard the emptiness. She filled her life, oh yes she did, but not with the kind of chemistry she felt with Adam, not with the kind of love she was beginning to feel for him, not with the personal connection so deep it could shake her soul.

She didn't think too long about what she was about to do. Rather, she just did it.

She went upstairs and showered with her favorite body wash. After she dried and curled her hair, she let it fall down her shoulders. No tying it back tonight. In the bottom of her underwear drawer, she found the lace undergarments in pale peach but then changed her mind and left them there. She put on a silky shirt dress she used for lounging around the house. With a pair of flats, she was all set.

Adam said she didn't have to call, so she didn't. She found a cream-colored poncho in the closet, swished it on over the dress and drove to his condo.

As she stood at Adam's door and rang his bell, she realized how he could go with the flow, how sometimes he seemed to like surprises. Had he expected her to show up tonight? And if she did, what did he expect to happen?

When Adam opened his door, she could decipher nothing from his expression. All he said was, "Glad you could come. I'll warm up the Chinese."

As she followed him through the living room, she realized she hadn't come here for a Chinese dinner.

"Is Erica asleep?" Her voice must have sounded just a tad shaky.

He studied her judiciously then responded, "She is. I put her down about a half hour ago. She should sleep a good three hours about now. At least that's the schedule she's been keeping."

Adam looked freshly showered. His gray T-shirt had a couple of dryer wrinkles. His black jeans fit him like jeans should. Was she really going to go through with this?

Through with what?

Through with letting desire win?

She dropped her purse onto a chair, then she slipped off her poncho and laid it across the back. "I'm not really hungry," she said. "At least not for Chinese."

Up until now his eyes had been an opaque green. The green deepened. Now there was male appreciation in his gaze as it drifted over her shirtdress. "You weren't wearing that at the community center."

No, she hadn't been. She had worn a button-down blouse and navy slacks under her cartoon lab coat.

"I stopped home to change," she said offhandedly.

"You don't usually wear your hair like that, either."

So he'd noticed. "It gets in the way like this when I'm working. That's why I tie it back."

He approached her slowly. "I like it like this. I like *you* like this." He swept his hand down the silky dress.

Silence invaded their space for a few moments. "I don't know how to do this, Adam."

He wasn't helping her out. "Do what?"

"Maybe we should just eat some Chinese," she said a bit defiantly.

With a deep chuckle, he came close enough to touch her. Then he did. Slipping his hand under her hair, he sifted his fingers through it, nudged her close, a few seconds later even closer.

When his lips pressed against hers, she expected coaxing. Everything about Adam always shouted finesse. This time there wasn't any finesse. It was only hunger and need. As his lips took hers, she knew this was what she'd wanted from that night at the winery. She'd been a coward that night. She'd been afraid of Adam's finesse and the fact that he probably knew too well how to turn a woman on. But now she knew who he was. Tonight she wanted what he offered, even if there was no future in it.

Her body heated up the longer he kissed her. A need grew inside her so big and great, no one could satisfy it but Adam. Their rocket-propelled passion had been gaining heat and velocity ever since the night they'd met.

Her arms went around his neck, and she could feel the beat of his heart as well as hers. The thumping primal beat urged her to savor the strength of his arms, the pads of his fingertips under her hair, the exciting matching of their bodies as they pressed together. When Adam rocked his hips against hers, she pushed back. She gave as good as she got. She was sure that's what he wanted, and it was what she wanted, too.

But then Adam did something that was totally Adam. He slowed it all down. He caressed her face. He held her cheeks in his hands.

"Is this what you want? Is this what you came here for tonight?" he asked, his voice husky and low.

"I want *you*. I want to touch and I want to be touched. For just once in my life, I want to live in the moment."

"This could be the second time in your life you did that." There was amusement in his voice, and she knew he was thinking about the first time they'd made love.

"For the second time, then, and who knows, maybe there will be a third."

He groaned. "You're killing me."

"That's not my intention."

"Show me your intention."

Sliding her fingers up his nape into this thick hair, she stood on tiptoe. But she didn't kiss him. Not exactly. She nibbled his upper lip and she ran her tongue over his lower lip. When she leaned her breasts into his chest, his control seemed to snap. His kiss was wild and so was her response. She wound her arms around his neck, wanting all of her doubts to go away by being totally invested in his kiss, totally invested in the moment. She almost forgot who she was. She forgot everything but passion.

His hands slid down her back and caressed her hips. The silky dress moved with each of the glides of his hands. His touch was thrilling, exciting, erotic. His hands grasped the material of her dress now, bunching it as if he wanted to pull it up and over her head. But she started shaking her head.

Breaking the kiss, she leaned back. "You have to unbutton it."

"You do know how to torture a man."

"You don't think it will be torture for *me* to wait for you to unfasten each button?"

Changing tactics, he kissed her neck and sucked her earlobe into his mouth. She really did feel like she was going to melt at his feet. Why hadn't she worn something with a zipper?

When he lifted his head again, his eyes were alight with a fire she felt, too. His fingers went to the first button at her neckline. "What do you have on under here?"

"Nothing," she said boldly.

"When were you going to tell me that?"

"I wasn't. I was going to let you discover it all on your own."

"You didn't tell me you were really a seductress at heart."

At heart? She was just a woman in love. But she certainly couldn't tell him *that*.

Time seemed to slow as her breaths became more shallow, as his breathing seemed to become more ragged. One button...two buttons...three buttons... four buttons. Finally the material seemed to part on its own and her breasts were revealed. The next thing she knew, he'd scooped her up into his arms and carried her to the sofa.

He sank to the sofa with her on his lap, his arms surrounding her. She was excited, yes, but most of all what she relished was the closeness, the knowledge that they were going to share something intimate. He unbuttoned a few more buttons, then bent his head to her breasts, taking her nipple into his mouth. Oh, yes, he was an expert. He knew what pleasure he could give. While he suckled one nipple, he played with the other, and she felt as if she'd come apart at the seams. Under her thighs she could feel his arousal. She could feel how much he wanted her. This is what had been missing in her marriage. This extreme sense of need and want on both their parts.

Almost every time she looked at Adam, her imagination created X-rated pictures. Was it the same with him?

"I want you naked," she demanded.

"That's a little hard right now," he said between kisses on her breasts. "I'm on the bottom."

She reached for his T-shirt. "Let's just start with your chest."

He laughed and leaned a little forward so she could grasp the material and pull it up over his head. It fell behind the sofa and neither of them cared.

"I do need my jeans for one thing," he said.

"What's that?"

"There's a condom in the pocket."

She leaned back slightly and stared him in the eyes. "You expected me to come over tonight?"

"I hoped you'd come. I certainly can't read your mind, Kaitlyn, but I *can* read desire. We both have it."

Heat was rolling off them in waves. Yes, they certainly had desire. But there was something in Adam's expression that told her he felt more than desire. Was she deluding herself?

As her dress fell to the floor, as she helped Adam

unbuckle his belt, she realized two things. Adam protected himself by not sinking into relationships…by not looking for anything long-term or serious. *She* protected herself by diving into her work. But tonight, as they got naked, it was as if they were peeling all that armor away.

Although they were both more than ready, Adam wouldn't hurry. He laid her back on the long sofa, stretched out on top of her and raised her hands above her head. "You're one beautiful woman. You're sexy no matter what you wear."

"Even in a cartoon-covered lab coat?" she joked.

"Even in that. You move like a dancer, so no matter what you're wearing, I just want to know and see what's underneath."

"I've never taken a dancing lesson," she said with a laugh.

"Some women have it, and some don't. You do."

He kissed her again to prove it. The kiss mirrored what he wanted to do with his body. She trembled as the yearning inside of her became a pulsing need. She couldn't keep still. She didn't want to keep still. She didn't want *him* to keep still.

"Adam, now," she said with a pant.

"Just a little longer…" He slid his hand up the inside of her thigh. He ran his thumb around her mound. He glided a finger inside of her, and she practically climaxed with that.

"Hold on to that thought," he growled in her ear, as he reached to the floor to his jeans, removed a packet and rolled on the condom.

"We can wait a little longer," he teased.

"Adam!"

Her tone was plaintive and scolding at the same time and he laughed. Then he wasn't laughing. He was rising above her, separating her legs, placing himself where she wanted him most. Pushing inside of her, he created circles of pleasurable sensations that kept spinning about her until she was dizzy. Each thrust wound the circles into each other until they coalesced into one, drawing tighter and tighter into itself until finally—

The winding coil broke, letting glorious sensations escape until heat suffused her body and tears rolled down her cheeks. Adam's release came seconds later, and he held on to her as if his climax had been as potent as hers.

Kaitlyn almost said the words then. She almost whispered, *I love you.* But in this one thing she held back. She was naked in every other way, and she couldn't reveal her deepest feelings, too.

Could Adam?

Their heartbeats had slowed a bit when he asked, "Are you okay?"

She was very okay—for the moment anyway. But isn't that all they were counting—the moments?

"I'm good. Wonderful in fact. How about you?"

"I think you're the single next best aphrodisiac after…chocolate."

She punched him and they both laughed.

Then he brushed her hair from her eyes and said, "Seriously, Kaitlyn, on a scale of one to ten, that was a twenty."

"Then maybe we should have Chinese and try for thirty." She didn't know what had gotten into her, but she was simply going to go with it.

"It just so happens, I bought a whole box of condoms."

Maybe by the time they used more than one, she'd get to the bottom of Adam's feelings for her.

And if she didn't? Then she'd just have to figure out the key that would unlock Adam Preston's heart.

Chapter Twelve

In a strange bed, wrapped in Adam's arms, Kaitlyn didn't quite recognize the noise the following morning when a gong sounded. It took a few minutes to realize it was Adam's doorbell.

They'd been up a few hours before with Erica. On a Sunday, Kaitlyn didn't have to rise as early as usual, so they hadn't set the alarm.

Adam murmured into her neck, "That could be my father for all I know. I'd better answer it, or he'll pound the door down next."

There was another gong.

"I should be getting up anyway," Kaitlyn said. "I have to make rounds at the hospital."

Adam buried his nose under her hair. "I had envisioned a morning of pancakes, maple syrup and lots of making out in between shaking a rattle at Erica. But..."

After another quick kiss to her cheek, he swung his legs off the side of the bed, slipped on a pair of jogging shorts and left the bedroom.

Kaitlyn quickly dressed, knowing she'd have to stop at her town house for clothes more appropriate to making hospital rounds. She kept one ear attuned to the living room. She didn't hear raised male voices, but she did hear—

Crying? A woman crying?

Erica was still sleeping in her crib in the sitting area of Adam's bedroom in that kind of early-morning sleep babies had. Her little fist was balled under her chin.

When Kaitlyn stepped into the living room, she found Adam sitting on the sofa with a young woman, his arm around her.

He looked up. "Tina's come home," he said, and made it a statement of fact.

Kaitlyn could tell he wasn't going to let his sister leave again, even if he had to tie her up and barricade her in his apartment.

"This is Kaitlyn," he said gently to his sister. "I think she left a message for you."

Tina, her honey-blond hair a bit disheveled, turned away from his shoulder and swiped at the tears on her cheek. "Your call on my phone was one of the reasons I came back."

Following her instincts, Kaitlyn sat on the long sofa on the other side of Adam's sister. "I'm glad my message made a difference."

"They all did," Tina admitted with a weak smile. "But I just had to be sure."

"Sure of what?" Adam asked, keeping his voice nonjudgmental.

"I missed Erica so much." She got choked up but then went on. "But I had to do what was best for her. I had to get my head on straight. I went to a clinic in San Jose. I talked to someone who said I had postpartum depression, and that lots of women get it, and that I shouldn't beat myself up, just get my life back on the right track."

"Sound advice," Adam said.

"You pretty much told me the same thing, but I guess I wasn't able to hear it. I mean, not about the postpartum depression, but about being overwhelmed and not seeing clearly. Anyway, the doctor put me on an antidepressant. He said it's temporary."

"It will help with the next few months," Kaitlyn agreed.

Yet there was a question hanging in the room, and Tina looked uncertain as she answered it. "I want to be Erica's mom. I want to take care of her again. But I don't know how or where or what will be best for her. If she starts crying again all the time and I don't know what to do for her, I'm afraid the same thing will happen. I can't cope."

Kaitlyn admired Tina's honesty. It was the same honesty she often felt from Adam. "When I left that message for you, I told you there is help of all kinds from The Mommy Club. We just have to figure out what you need. The first step will be to find a doctor in Fawn Grove, and you can start attending the new moms' group."

"For now, you'll stay here with me," Adam said. "I've turned into good dad material and I can show you the ropes. Erica was on the wrong formula and that's why she was crying all the time. There are ways to end her restlessness, too." He motioned to the swing. "She loves that. Taking care of her won't be easy, but if you *want* to be a mom—"

"Oh, I do. I looked at the pictures you sent about fifty times a day. Can I see her now?"

Adam quickly rose from the sofa. "I'll get her."

In a few minutes he was back with Erica swaddled in a blanket. Her little eyes were just coming open.

"Here's your daughter," he said to his sister and placed the baby in her arms.

From the expression on Tina's face, Kaitlyn suspected Adam's sister wasn't going to leave her daughter ever again.

After hospital rounds, Kaitlyn headed toward Fawn Grove's family diner—Country Comfort. She didn't want to meet Tom, but she'd set up lunch with him at a neutral place. Tina and her brother needed time together. She hadn't wanted to interfere in their family unit. Maybe Adam hadn't had many ties when he was growing up, but he certainly had a bond with his sister. After taking care of Erica, she doubted whether he'd ever be out of contact with Tina again.

When Kaitlyn reached the diner, Tom was already sitting in a booth. She slid in on the other side, face-to-face, eye-to-eye. She realized whatever he thought or whatever he did no longer had the power to hurt her or change her life. That really was a freeing feeling.

Before she could even say hello, he said, "I overreacted."

Relieved that's how they were starting, she admitted, "I'm sorry I didn't warn you about the interview. I honestly didn't think it would be any more invasive than what I wrote for the newspaper. I should have known better."

Tom played with his fork for a few minutes then said, "I don't think it was the miscarriage that ended our marriage."

"No?" she asked, wanting to hear what he had to say.

"No. I think I had a lot of resentment built up and it all poured out over that. You know, like, when there's an argument about how to load the dishwasher, but it's really not about the dishwasher."

Oh, yes, she knew exactly what he meant, but she remained silent, because he seemed to need to get this off his chest.

"I just couldn't get used to the idea that I wasn't the center of your world. Your dedication to your career was."

"I didn't know how to do it any other way," she confessed. "Being a doctor meant everything to me. I thought I had to be the best doctor in the world to prove something to myself and to make my parents proud. Maybe I'm still trying to prove something to my father."

"The Christmas card dad?" Tom asked with a wise grimace.

He'd called her father that because that was the only time she heard from him. She received a Christmas card over the holidays.

"After I lost the baby, I blamed myself as much as you did."

He nodded. "I know. I should have helped you somehow, but I didn't know how."

"Time was an important factor. I needed time."

The waitress came to their table and took their orders. Afterward, Tom asked, "So who was the guy and the baby?"

"His name is Adam Preston. Erica is his sister's baby. She just returned from out of town."

"Is it serious?"

Kaitlyn hesitated. Especially after last night, *it* was serious on her part. But she didn't know how Adam felt about that. Now that Tina was home, he'd certainly be leaving on schedule.

"You don't have to say anything else," her ex-husband said. "I hope it works out for you."

She could see Tom really did wish her well. She just wasn't sure what "working out" meant.

To Kaitlyn's surprise, when she arrived at Adam's that afternoon, Sara was there. She'd told her friend Tina had returned...and Sara was on the spot. Right away, Kaitlyn saw that Tina was holding Erica, and she had a feeling she'd been doing that as much as she could since she'd returned.

The look Adam gave her said he'd missed her. She wanted to wrap her arms around his neck and give him a huge kiss. Yet the truth was, she didn't really know where they stood. What was going to happen next?

"Sara made Tina an offer I don't think she can refuse," Adam explained.

Sara grinned at them all. "Our guest cottage at Raintree is just sitting there empty. Amy and I loved it when we stayed there. So...I came over to invite Tina and Erica to live there. Jase, Amy, Ethan and I will be right across the lane, and Liam's above the winery. It's a beautiful location for walks and toddling around as Erica gets bigger. Marissa's around a lot with Jordan, too, so I don't think you'd get lonely," she said to Tina. "What do you think?"

"Adam asked me if I wanted to stay *here* while he was gone," Tina said.

"Once you see that guest cottage, you're going to want to stay *there*," he responded.

"But my job's in Sacramento, and I really can't afford to lose it. I need to pay my way," Tina assured them all.

Sara nodded. "I understand. I felt the same way as a single mom. What if you could get a job here in Fawn Grove?"

"That would be perfect," Tina agreed.

"Jase deals with lawyers all the time in the winery business. I'm sure he'll check around, if that's what you really want."

Tina looked at all of them, and maybe finally she realized this was a group that was going to give her support. She wasn't alone anymore. "If he hears of a job here in Fawn Grove, I'll take it."

While Sara and Tina talked about the guest cottage, Adam pulled Kaitlyn into the kitchen. "So how did it go with your ex?"

"It went very well."

Adam scowled. "And just what does that mean?"

Could he be jealous? "It means we talked. He told me how he felt, and I listened. He wished me well."

"No follow-up dinners?" Adam asked.

"No follow-up dinners," she assured him.

Adam wrapped his arm around her and pulled her away from the doorway into the small breakfast nook, where Tina and Sara couldn't see them. Then he gave her a hard, long, deep, wet kiss that curled her toes and maybe her hair, too.

Afterward, he said in a low voice, "I don't know when we're going to be alone again. This move into the guest cottage will be good for Tina, but I want to make sure she's ready to live there alone with Erica and take care of her."

"Sara and Jase will watch over her, and I will, too," Kaitlyn assured him.

"I guess you don't skip out for a couple of hours for an afternoon delight?" he asked hopefully.

"It's possible I could meet you at my place for an hour over lunch, if you can be flexible."

"Flexible is how I live my life," he maintained with a grin. "Tomorrow?"

"Tomorrow. I'll call you when I'm free."

"Call me when you're on the way to the town house so I can get there at the same time."

She laughed. This wasn't like her at all, and she still didn't know what came next. But for now, an hour with Adam tomorrow would have to do.

On Sunday, a week later, Kaitlyn dropped her overnight bag onto the floor in Adam's bedroom, acutely aware of the package inside. It was a pregnancy test and it was time to use it. Her period was over a week late. Only, she wanted to wait until morning when the results would be the most effective.

Morning. Her life could change because of a message on a stick.

Couldn't her life change tonight as well, if Adam told her how he felt? She'd spent the past week enjoying every moment they could steal together. They were both pushing the knowledge he was leaving next weekend into the recesses of their minds. At least *she* was. Was he looking forward to flying off again?

This weekend had been tough on him. They'd moved Tina into Sara and Jase's guesthouse today. She knew he hadn't wanted to leave Tina alone there with Erica, but he had. She was sure he'd be checking in with her every couple of hours until Tina got tired of the interference and told him to stop.

Or maybe she wouldn't. A renewed connection with an older brother wasn't something to mess with.

When Kaitlyn went into the living room, she found Adam standing by a side table, a tiny bib in his hand, a remnant of Erica's stay here.

She came up behind him and wrapped her arms around his waist. Peering over his shoulder, she said, "You can drop it off tomorrow."

He turned around and shook his head. "I didn't realize how hard it was going to be to leave her there."

"Erica or Tina?"

"Both. I know Sara and Jase are right there."

"And Liam and Ethan. Sara says under his lady-killer ways, Liam's a good guy. Stop worrying until there's something to worry about."

Adam let the bib drop to the table, and he gave her a small smile. "I've watched her handle Erica all week and she seems to have the hang of it. Sleep deprivation will probably be the biggest problem. I know it was for me."

Spoken like a dad, Kaitlyn thought. What if he

was a dad? To distract herself from that thought for the moment, she reminded him, "Erica's sleeping for longer stretches now and that should help. She's satisfied on the formula, and Tina seems to like playing with her, counting toes and fingers. We stocked the refrigerator, and Sara invited her for dinner tonight."

"The job Jase heard about seems like a good fit—a paralegal secretary for a general law office."

"What more could you want?" Kaitlyn teased, and realized how much more *she* wanted. She wanted Adam to stay. She wanted a life with him. But all they had now was an affair and that's what he was used to.

"What are we going to do for dinner?" he asked with an arched brow.

"Sara invited *us,* too."

"Yes, she did, but then I would have lost a whole evening with you. I wasn't going to give *that* up."

She knew that look in his eye. She could feel the sexual tension now stringing his body. She wanted tonight as much as he did, because they didn't know how many nights they'd have.

"Do you have much preparation for your trip?" she asked.

"Lots of emails, scanned documents zipping back and forth. I've met the team through video conferencing. There will be more of that this week, but I really don't want to talk about that. Do you?"

No, she didn't. Her hunger for Adam seemed to exceed everything else in her life. That was so unusual, and it scared her sometimes.

When Adam lowered his head to kiss her, she was eager for it. His tongue immediately played across her lips, seeking entrance. She responded to his foray, feeling transported as she always did. His tongue found the inside of her cheek, explored a bit, and repetitively stroked against her. Her knees began to wobble, and her whole body trembled.

Adam had taught her what passion was really about. He'd taught her how two people could want and need and satisfy. Yet not really satisfy. Not ever. Not unless there was a lifetime of passion and a lifetime of joining hearts. She wanted to do more than join her body to his. She wanted to join their hearts.

Their kisses became more fevered. He broke away, saying, "The bedroom is always so far away."

"Why do we need the bedroom?" she asked provocatively. "Don't you always carry a condom in your pocket for our fast-food lunches?"

Their quickies at her place were exciting, a bit forbidden and altogether fulfilling. So fulfilling, in fact, that the receptionist at the office had asked her what new makeup she was using to give her that glow.

Adam's lovemaking gave her that glow.

Adam breathed into her neck, inhaling her fragrance, as his hand went to the edge of her top. But after he had it up and over her head and tossed it to the floor, he took her face between his palms and kissed her deeply. Kaitlyn didn't even care about his shirt. Her fingers pulled at the recalcitrant leather of his belt and undid it.

"Eager, aren't we?" he asked with a chuckle.

She answered by unzipping his fly and caressing him.

He groaned. "You do know how to get a man revved up. Let's see if I can do the same thing to you."

Sliding his hand to her waist, he unfastened her jeans, pushed them down and cupped her bottom. He kissed between her cleavage, unfastened her bra and bent his head to her breasts.

But then he said, "Let's make this easier. Take off your jeans and I'll do the same."

Easier? She wasn't sure about that, but she wanted to get her clothes off as much as he did his. He was already done until she slipped out of her jeans. Taking her by the waist, he lifted her up on the table.

"Better access," he muttered, as he bent to her breasts again and explored one nipple while he flicked the other.

She was wriggling and restless now, ready for him. But he seemed to have more pleasure planned for her. He stroked her thighs apart until she was panting and reaching for him. He just laughed and kept on, using his fingers to flutter against her...using his fingertips in inventive ways that made her breath catch.

"Adam…"

"Soon," he crooned, his voice deep and husky, alerting her he was almost ready, too.

He touched her where he knew she'd feel sparks and sensations that would throw her into climax. She didn't want to go without him. Yet, everything he was doing was so deliciously wonderful. She said his name again, and this time he must have agreed that both of them were more than ready.

She opened her eyes when she heard the foil packet tear. She reached out and took it from him, and smoothed it over him, making him groan. Holding her hips, he brought her closer to the edge of the table and then he thrust in, once, twice, three times, until the pleasure was so great she didn't know if she could stand it. Each time they made love, it got better. Each time they made love, she fell deeper in love with him. Each time they made love, she dreamed of a future. His drives into her increased in speed and intensity until she was at the breaking point and so was he.

"Come with me," he commanded Kaitlyn, and she easily obeyed the command. Adam's loving took her over the highest crest she'd ever experienced. She wanted to stay on top of that pleasurable wave and ride it forever.

She wanted to love Adam forever.

He held on to her and she held on to him. When their hearts had fallen to a more normal rhythm, he looked down at her, kissed her forehead, wrapped his arms around her and sighed.

"After that fantastic expenditure of energy, we can do one of two things," he advised her.

"What two are you thinking of?"

"We can make omelets for supper, or we can get a shower together."

They'd never done that, and every first with Adam was spectacular.

"I suppose this just wouldn't be a normal shower?"

"Not if I have anything to say about it." He wriggled his brows.

She laughed, but the laughter faded as she thought about the package in her duffel bag. Tomorrow morning would be time enough to think about that.

Kaitlyn slipped out of Adam's bed the next morning and grabbed her nightgown from the floor beside the bed, knowing what she had to do. If Adam came in and saw what she was doing, so be it. Then that was meant to be. She'd put her duffel in the bathroom the night before, so she could easily access the package. Now she took it from its wrappings, read the instructions, which she was already familiar with, and went about the task of finding out whether or not she was pregnant. Five minutes later, her nightgown on and her teeth brushed, she stared at the wand in her hand, disbelieving.

Oh, she'd known pregnancy was a possibility, but really, what were the odds?

Apparently the odds were 100 percent that she and Adam had created a baby. But now what was she going to do? Tell him right away? Wait and see if he expressed what he was feeling before he left for Thailand? Would that make a difference?

Of course it would. She wouldn't trap him in something he didn't want. After one failed marriage, she knew everything would have to be right to enter into one again. Marriage might not even be in the cards. Did Adam feel for her what she felt for him?

She was still debating what she should do when Adam called in from the bedroom. "Kaitlyn, your cell's ringing. Do you want me to get it?"

"I'm coming."

Hurriedly she pushed everything about the pregnancy test back into the bag and stuffed it into her duffel. This early on Monday morning it could be the hospital calling, or even another doctor in her practice. Hurrying into the bedroom, she reached for her phone on the nightstand and answered the call.

"Dr. Foster here."

As she glanced around Adam's room, she noticed something she hadn't noticed last night. He had a pile of clothes stacked on top of the chest. It looked like a stack of work clothes—khakis and cargo pants, sweatshirts, T-shirts, and on the floor beside the chest stood sturdy boots. She guessed he was assembling his wardrobe to take to Thailand. She hadn't caught sight of it last night because she'd been so mesmerized with him and what they were doing…the pleasure they could give each other. But now in the light of day, she could see the truth more clearly. He *was* going to leave.

When the voice on the other end of the line said, "Dr. Foster, I'm sorry to call so early, but I wanted to make sure I got you. My name is Bernadette Mathis. I'm with The Mommy Club Foundation in San Jose."

The post office box Marissa sent the money to had an address in San Jose.

"I see," Kaitlyn said, not seeing at all. "Is there some way I can help you?"

"Yes, indeed there is. We saw the interview you did with Tanya Edwards."

Kaitlyn wondered who the "we" was. "Yes?"

"You did a wonderful job with it. The viewing public was obviously touched by your story because donations are rolling in."

"I'm happy about that. That means we can help more families."

"Exactly, and that's my point. Up until now, The Mommy Club has been kept to a local level in Fawn Grove. But the founder is thinking about expanding statewide. After all, as you said, every community could use a Mommy Club. So we have a question for you. Would you consider being our spokesperson, letting a PR consultant find you spots on statewide talk shows and the like?"

The offer threw Kaitlyn completely off balance. "I don't know," she said.

"I'd like you to come to San Jose and meet with me about it. I know you're a busy woman, and you have a practice, but we can be flexible in our time frame. What do you think?"

Kaitlyn wasn't sure exactly what to think. After all, she just found out she was pregnant. "Can I have twenty-four hours to think about it?"

"Sure, you can. You have my number on your phone now?"

"I'll send it to my contact list."

"All right, then I expect to hear from you in a day or so."

After Kaitlyn said a goodbye, she saw Adam was watching her. He was naked and rumpled and oh, so sexy.

She gave a little shrug. "That was unexpected."

"Something you have to think about for twenty-four hours?"

"The Mommy Club Foundation representative wants me to go to San Jose and meet with her. She thinks I'd be a good spokesperson. They want to book me on some talk shows."

"You can't *seriously* be thinking about it."

"Of course I'm seriously thinking about it. This could be important for The Mommy Club."

"I can't believe you want to take on something else."

She heard judgment in his tone, just as she'd once

heard it with Tom. She said simply, "You've no right to judge my life when you're going to be leaving."

"That sounds like a judgment of *my* life."

"Then maybe we both ought to back off," she said, hurt he couldn't express his feelings toward her, worried most that he didn't want to be a husband or life partner, let alone a dad.

"Maybe we should," he agreed, going to the bedside chair and gathering up a pair of running shorts. He stepped into them. They rode low, just under his navel. "It looks as if you're going to be busy with two careers, and I'm not going to be in the country," he added in a measured tone.

Suddenly she felt like crying. That couldn't be hormones already, could it? And she certainly wouldn't cry in front of *him*.

She'd hung her outfit for today in his closet, and now she went for it. "I have to get going. I have to make rounds."

He caught her arm. "Does this mean I won't be seeing you again before I leave?"

Oh, how she wanted to keep seeing him. She wanted more nights like last night in his arms, in his condo, in his life. But she wasn't in his life if he was going to leave expecting to return to an affair.

"Would there be any point?" she asked sadly.

His mouth tightened and his jaw set. He released her arm. "Maybe not."

Avoiding his gaze, she took her clothes into the bathroom and shut the door.

She was in shock, that was all. Learning she was pregnant was enough to do that. Figuring out what to do about Adam was the rest of it. She was so confused.

And as far as the job as spokesperson?

She'd figure that out after she absorbed the fact she was going to be a mom and her baby's dad would be a world away.

Chapter Thirteen

On one hand, Kaitlyn felt the joy of new life growing inside of her. She was going to pay attention to every detail this time. She'd understand every change in her body, eat right, exercise and somehow make sure she didn't overdo.

But her heart hurt because Adam was flying away from Fawn Grove tomorrow. He was flying away from the two of them. While he was gone, she'd figure out how to tell him about the baby. She'd figure out if she could handle him being in her life only sometimes. That wasn't what she wanted, but she'd learned a long time ago, a girl couldn't always get what she wanted.

Sara was arranging her notes on the podium. This was a workshop about volunteering to help in The Mommy Club, and Sara would be talking about the strength and scope of their work, too.

Kaitlyn was sitting at the table beside the podium, her notes, a list of Mommy Club services, and handouts spread out in front of her. As the group trickled in the door, she noticed mostly women taking seats. Dads could use help, too. Like Adam.

Adam.

"What's the matter?" Sara asked, as she went to stand beside Kaitlyn. "You look so sad."

Suddenly Kaitlyn found it hard to speak and she swallowed hard. "I'm going to miss him."

"Of course you are. How did you leave it?" Sara asked in a low voice.

"We sort of had an argument, then we just left it. But I—"

She almost said she was pregnant, but she couldn't tell anybody about that, not until Adam knew. It wouldn't be fair.

"So you didn't tell him how you feel?"

"No, for lots of reasons."

"You really should consider if any of them are good enough. I mean it, Kaitlyn."

"But what if he doesn't feel anything back?" Kaitlyn asked in almost a whisper.

"Then you'll know. Isn't that better than second-guessing? Isn't that better than worrying about what's going to happen when he comes back?"

She still had time. Adam wasn't leaving until tomorrow. She could go to him this afternoon after the workshop. She could tell him he didn't have to say anything. She could tell him he could think about everything while he was gone. She could tell him—

She loved him.

Turning, she looked up at Sara.

"Maybe you're right. Maybe that's exactly what I should do. I've been so torn by doubts all week. I'm still afraid, though. How do you prepare yourself for taking that kind of risk?"

"There's no preparation. All you can do is listen to your heart and follow it."

Follow your heart. She'd followed her heart into medicine. She'd followed her heart into The Mommy Club. Now could she follow her heart to Adam?

About fifteen women had come into the room and were now seated in the folding chairs.

"We should get started," Kaitlyn said. She'd dropped her tote bag with handouts, name tags and the like under the table at her feet. But it had gotten pushed down out of her reach. She stood quickly then stooped over to retrieve it. When she did, she suddenly felt light-headed. Black dots swam before her eyes. She felt so odd, so…

The gray dots became a gray veil that took her down to the floor.

Adam watched Tina change Erica into a Onesie embroidered with two kittens. She did it easily with a tickle at her baby's tummy and a finger rub along the side of her daughter's cheek.

Glancing at the walls of the baby's room in the guesthouse at Raintree Winery, he saw there were large decals of baby ducks and young horses, puppies and cats arranged on them.

"It looks as if you've settled in."

"I have, and everyone's been so helpful. I never knew there was a network like this. Maybe if I had…"

"You wouldn't have felt so alone?"

Her straight blond hair slipping over her shoulder, she gazed at him with wide gray eyes. "You do understand, don't you?"

"After caring for Erica when I didn't know what I was doing, I understand. If it hadn't been for Kaitlyn—" As soon as he said it, he buried the thought and any others that came with it.

Tina lifted her baby into her arms, cooed into her neck and settled her on her shoulder. "Kaitlyn called me yesterday to check in."

"Did she?" The tone of his voice said he didn't want to go on with the conversation.

His sister must have understood that, because she said, "George called, too. He and Iris are honeymooning by playing roulette and taking in shows, but they're flying back from Vegas next week."

His father hadn't told him that.

Tina went on, "He said he and Iris want to take me to dinner and he asked to spend a little time with Erica."

Had his father taken his words to heart? "How do you feel about that?"

Tina shrugged. "I've always liked George. He used to show me his coin collection, explaining where each one came from, and sometimes how they were made. The gold ones fascinated me and he told me those are the ones I should keep."

Adam laughed. "*That's* true enough."

With a little shrug, Tina commented, "I came to understand my mom wanted a homebody, and he wasn't. He always wanted to be on the move and traveling, seeing new things and going new places."

"Jade wanted security and stability for you."

Looking down at her daughter lovingly, Tina rubbed her back. "I suppose so. And we had it for a few years. That's better than not at all. They were so different. I don't know what they saw in each other from the beginning, but who can explain chemistry?"

Adam thought about the bags packed at the door of his condo, about his flight tomorrow, about everything but the feelings rolling around inside of him.

"So are you and Kaitlyn going to keep in touch while you're gone?" Tina asked.

Not the way they'd left it last weekend. "I don't know," he muttered.

"With video conferencing you could have virtual sex long-distance."

"Tina."

His sister laughed. "I know the score, Adam. You and Kaitlyn sizzle when you're in the same room. There's no reason you can't keep the fire sizzling while you're gone. Then when you come back—"

"That's not what Kaitlyn wants."

"Do you *know* what she wants?"

He knew what Kaitlyn *didn't* want. She didn't want an on-again, off-again relationship. She didn't simply want a hot affair—which is what they'd had. It was the "had" that bothered him. It was the "had" that had kept him awake every night. It was the "had" that was making him reevaluate how he was living and what he wanted going forward.

He'd told Jase that he loved the work but that traveling was getting old. What if he *did* make a change? What if he took that professorship at Wilson and maybe did consulting work on the side?

As he and Tina went to the living room, he mulled it all over.

"Do you want to hold her for a few minutes while I get her bottle ready?" she asked.

"Of course," he responded with a wide smile, naturally scooping his niece into his arms. He was going to miss *this,* too.

Adam's cell phone beeped from his belt. Transferring Erica to the crook of his arm, he reached for it, knowing this could be about his trip…or the project. But when he checked caller ID, he saw Sara Cramer's number.

Tina had finished preparing Erica's bottle. Crossing to Adam, she took Erica from him and sat on the sofa to feed her.

Adam answered the call. "Hi, Sara," he said, wondering if she was over at the house.

"Kaitlyn doesn't know I'm calling. She passed out while she was giving a workshop."

"Passed out?" he almost shouted. "Where are you?"

"Fortunately this place is crawling with doctors. Her gynecologist is seeing her now."

"Her gynecologist?"

"That's the doctor she asked me to call. I was ready to dial 9-1-1, but when she came to, she said she wanted to see Dr. Morelli."

A tightening began in Adam's chest and spread through his body. "How long was she out?"

"She says she wasn't, and everything just got fuzzy and she was dizzy."

"She's in the building where her practice is?"

"Suite 201."

"I'll be there in ten minutes. Don't let her leave."

"This is Kaitlyn, Adam."

He shook his head. "Yes, I know. But maybe she'll be shaken up enough to listen to reason."

He ended the call, shut his phone and said to Tina, "I've got to go. Kaitlyn passed out when she was giving a workshop."

"If you need moral support, I can come along. Erica's portable."

He almost smiled. "I know she is, and thank you for offering. This, I've got to do on my own."

"What's 'this'?" Tina asked.

"This" was taking shape in his mind. "This" was a feeling for Kaitlyn that couldn't be denied. "This" was concern and worry and the urge to wrap his arms around her and protect her forever. "This" was what he was going to explain to her and hope she felt the same way.

Adam rushed to Suite 201, unmindful of bystanders and other patients he passed when he jogged through the hall. All he cared about was getting to Kaitlyn. All he cared about was finding out if she was okay. All he cared about was telling her—

That he didn't want on-again, off-again. He was thinking about forever instead of a trip to Thailand. Just how was she going to react to that? Especially after the way they'd left it. Would she trust him? Would she believe in *them*?

Sara met Adam in the waiting room of the gynecologist's office suite.

"Where is she?"

"She's talking with her doctor. She's probably going to be angry I called you."

"I don't care how angry she is. I want to go back there."

Fortunately, he didn't have to storm the doctor's office. Kaitlyn was walking down the hall toward him, looking a little paler than she usually did. But other than that, she seemed to be moving on her own steam, and he wondered if she *should* be.

Adam met her at the reception window. There wasn't anyone there.

Kaitlyn eyed him, looking surprised. "What are you doing here?"

"I called him," Sara confessed, not looking sorry at all.

Still, Kaitlyn gave her a scolding look.

But Sara just waved her hand. "I'm going back to Raintree. The workshop is canceled for today. We'll reschedule it. Everybody understands that things happen."

"What *thing* happened?" Adam asked.

Kaitlyn gave Sara a hug. "I'll talk to you soon."

Without another word, Sara simply gave Adam a wink. He didn't know what that was supposed to mean, but he took that it meant she approved of him being here.

Taking Kaitlyn by the arm, he guided her toward one of the chairs in the reception area. "Sit," he commanded.

For once she didn't argue with him.

"The workshop?" he prompted. "Why did you end up here?"

She waved her hand. "Low blood pressure. It sometimes happens when— Adam, I have something to tell you."

"I have something to tell *you* first." Sitting down beside her, he took her hands into his.

"I've been doing a lot of thinking this past week on a lot of fronts. Actually I've been doing a lot of thinking the past month."

"Because of Tina disappearing?"

"Tina disappearing…and meeting *you*. Whether you know it or not, Kaitlyn, you've changed the way I look at the world. I see it through maybe kinder eyes. Sure, my profession and work helps people, but certainly not the way you do. Your one-on-one caring has affected me in ways I never imagined. And to top it all off, when Dad came back, he made me realize I want to be different than he is. I don't want five marriages. I only want *one*."

Kaitlyn's eyes were wide now with astonishment, and maybe with hope. He was praying he saw hope.

"I love you, Kaitlyn. I may have been slow coming to realize it. I may have called it passion instead of love, but it's so much more than desire."

"Adam…"

He didn't know what she was going to say, but he had to finish. He had to lay it all on the table. He had to bare his heart and soul and hope that vulnerability would be enough.

"I not only love you, Kaitlyn, I want to marry you. I want to have a life with you. With Erica, I've seen that I can be a good dad. I'm bringing all my newly learned skills to the table," he joked, though he didn't feel like joking. "Will you marry me?"

He could see the tears in Kaitlyn's eyes, and the emotion she was trying to contain. He wasn't sure exactly why she was trying to contain it. He waited for her answer but one didn't come.

Instead, she squeezed his hands. "There's something I have to tell you."

She'd said that once before, and now he listened, suddenly afraid. What if she was going to tell him she was going back to her ex-husband? She'd said that was over, but—

Looking directly into his eyes, as if she was trying to see to the bottom of his soul, she said, "Adam, I'm pregnant."

It only took a second for him to absorb what she'd said. It was so different from what he'd almost expected. But he gave out a whoop, stood and then swung her up into his arms. "You're pregnant?"

"Yes," she said shakily. "I just found out last Sunday. But then we had that sort of argument, and I thought you just wanted to fly away."

He held her tighter. "I don't want to fly away. That's the whole point. Wilson University offered me that professorship anytime I wanted it. I'm going to accept it. I'm going to do some scrambling to find someone to take over for me in Thailand, but I can do it because I want to stay here and make a life. I want to stay here and be an uncle to Erica and a brother to Tina. I want the connections I've run away from all my life. But most of all, I want to settle down with the woman I love. With you…and a baby."

She laughed and repeated, "A baby."

"And you fainted from low blood pressure?"

"Apparently it happens. I stood up quickly, stooped over even quicker, and everything went black. My doctor checked me out and everything's okay. I'll probably worry every step of the way because of the last time."

"You're not going to be worrying alone. Instead of worrying, we're going to think something positive every time we do. We're going to take good care of you and the baby."

"*We* are?"

"Yes, *we* are. Are you going to take this spokesperson position with The Mommy Club?"

"I thought about it long and hard, and here's what I've come up with. With this pregnancy, I want to take good care of myself. So I've talked with the practice about going part-time. That would also be good when I go back to work after the baby's born. If I'm part-time, I can easily take a spokesperson assignment once every couple of weeks. That's sort of what I ironed out with The Mommy Club Foundation's representative. What do you think?"

"I think it's smart. I think all of it's going to play into your strengths. I'll help you any way I can."

"I haven't told you the one thing I was going to tell you before you flew off. I was going to come see you this afternoon, after the workshop."

"What did you want to tell me?"

"That I love you. That I think I started loving you that first night we met at the winery. Oh, I put the brakes on because I knew getting involved with you would probably rock my life, and it has. But in the best way possible. I love you, Adam Preston."

His arms around her, he pulled her even closer. "Can we get married sooner rather than later?"

"We can get married as soon as you and the state of California allow."

"You want a dress, don't you? Bridesmaids? A church?"

"I don't need a princess gown, just something I like and that you'll think I look beautiful in. As far as bridesmaids—Marissa, Sara and Tina. I'd like to keep it simple if we can."

"Would you like to have it at Raintree?"

"Sara and Jase's wedding was at Raintree, and it was beautiful. We can keep it intimate, have a harpist, an elegant ceremony Marissa can help plan. She's good at that."

"As soon as possible," he decreed. "We've put the cart before the horse, and I want to get caught up. I don't want our child to put two and two together too easily when it comes to his birth."

"Or her birth. A girl would want to know every detail."

"Are you saying a boy would be oblivious?"

"I'm not sure. I guess we'll find out. Do you think your dad will come?"

"I don't think he'd miss it. You have a lot of friends, Kaitlyn. How are we going to keep it small and intimate?"

"Intimate has to do with the setting and a state of mind and the way the ceremony's handled. If we keep the guest list to seventy-five or a hundred, I think we'll be okay. I know we'll be okay because the kind of wedding we have simply doesn't matter. What matters is what we do *after* the wedding."

"You mean the honeymoon?" he asked, kissing the tip of her nose.

"*After* the honeymoon."

"Let's not skip the pleasure of the honeymoon. Where do you want to go?"

"I've always wanted to spend time in Carmel."

He swung her up off the floor and held her tight. "Then Carmel it is."

Laughing, she asked, "Are you going to grant my every wish?"

"Every wish within reason. That's what we can do for each other."

She took his face between her hands. "And just what would your first wish be?"

"That you'll spend every day and night with me."

"We won't get anything done!"

"Sure, we will. I can teach, and we can work together on Mommy Club projects. You can be a spokesperson, and I'll drive you to and from your events. You can be a doctor. When you come home, we'll have dinner and talk about our day. On the odd weekend we have nothing to do, we can drive somewhere and have another honeymoon. At least until the baby's born. We'll make this work, Kaitlyn. I promise we will."

"I have no doubt we'll make it work, because I love you and you love me."

"And baby will make three."

Then Adam bent his head and gave her the gentlest, yet most seductive kiss of their courtship. It was a promise that when they got married they'd make everything work—for all of them. Because their love was going to be so big, and so wide, and so high, that it would surround everyone they knew. It would touch everyone they knew.

After the kiss, Adam rested his forehead against hers. "Your town house or my condo?"

"How about a place of our own?"

"I second that." Then he kissed her again.

Epilogue

"Don't open your eyes," Adam commanded as he guided Kaitlyn across a wide porch to the door of a house he hoped she'd like.

"I can't open my eyes. You have your hands over them," she pointed out with a laugh.

"My hands could slip but I don't want you to see until we're inside. Just lift your foot up over the doorstep, and we're there. Or I could carry you—"

"You already carried me over the threshold to our honeymoon suite in Sacramento, and over the threshold of each hotel room as we drove along the coast. I think I can manage to step over this one."

The wedding had been perfect—Kaitlyn dressed in white satin; him in a tux; Sara, Marissa and Tina in cocktail dresses of their choosing. Since they'd wanted to get married quickly, they'd kept everything simple, yet meaningful. He remembered his vows. He remembered Kaitlyn's.

"What makes you think this is the right house?" she asked.

"You'll see," he assured her, and led her inside. Once inside the living room, he took his hands from her eyes.

She blinked then slowly looked around. The living room had a vaulted ceiling with beautiful wood beams. The plank flooring had a rustic look. A floor-to-ceiling native rock fireplace was the centerpiece in the room.

"Oh, Adam."

In front of the fireplace sat a caned-back rocking chair. On it was a four-foot teddy bear with a big blue bow around its neck.

Kaitlyn walked toward it, her smile tremulous. "It looks perfect there," she said softly.

"I thought so, too. And check the view out the window. On a clear day, you can probably see Raintree Winery. But no matter what, you can see those mountains in the distance."

"You listened to everything I said, everything I wanted." Her voice caught and he knew Kaitlyn was full of the emotion that he felt, too.

"Thanksgiving is almost here."

"Do you think we can be moved by then?" Kaitlyn asked.

"If we sign the contract on the house today, if we get all of our friends to help us, if we can find a table big enough for Dad and Iris, Tina and Erica and the two of us."

"And soon there will be three."

Adam laid his hand on Kaitlyn's tummy. "And soon there will be three. I love you."

"I love you, too."

He could see the bottomless world of it in her eyes, and he knew their future would be filled with a lot of happy and forever after.

* * * * *

M